To Jordan,
Sarah, A̶_____ and Chloe;
Lloyd and Neville.

● BARTER BOOKS ●
ALNWICK STATION
NORTHUMBERLAND

1

'Nooooooo Mummy, I don't want to go!' screamed Rosa.

Mum sighed.

Standing in the hallway, surrounded by suitcases, I wanted to scream out, but I could see that Mum was tired and she didn't know what to do.

'You have to go, Rosa, Donelle will be with you.' She hugged Rosa tightly. Rosa continued to cry.

How can you explain to a four-year-old that her mother has to go into hospital and that she and her ten-year-old sister would have to stay with an aunt?

'I don't want to go, Mummy. Can't Jas look after us?' whined Donelle.

Mum picked up Rosa and, turning to Donelle, she said, 'Don't you start, I've explained to you and Jasmine about a hundred times why you have to go away. Just don't make it any harder for me.'

She took Rosa upstairs.

'Want a drink, Donelle?' I asked.

'Yeah, why not? It'll be my last one in this house for ages.'

I couldn't answer her. We walked into the kitchen. Donelle sat at the table while I opened the fridge and got out some fruit juice.

Sensing the tears welling up in my eyes I pretended to sneeze. 'Achoo. Oh, my eyes.'

'Hayfever,' slurped Donelle.

'Yeah.' It was May. A bit early for hayfever but I'd rather

1

Donelle thought it was hayfever than realise that I was crying.

We were just finishing off the carton of juice when the doorbell rang.

Upstairs, Rosa screamed.

Tears sprang out of Donelle's eyes.

I felt sick.

I opened the door to Aunt Merri who beamed, nearly blinding me with her sparkling white teeth.

'Hi Aunt Merri.' I grinned weakly.

'Hello Jasmine. You've grown so tall.' She hugged me. I knew what was coming next.

'What have you done to your hair? Let me see.'

I turned around dutifully for her – it was no use protesting.

'Why did your mother let you shave off all your beautiful hair and only leave a little turf on the top? And you've bleached that. It looks terrible against your cinnamon complexion. Oh my goodness.'

Mum came down the stairs carrying Rosa. I took that as my cue to slip up the stairs into my room.

Closing the door behind me, I threw myself on to my bed and put my hands over my ears – I didn't want to hear what was going on downstairs.

I couldn't say goodbye to my sisters, even though I would hardly be seeing them over the next three months. Breaking down in front of them just before they were taken away wouldn't have left them with a good impression.

'Come and say goodbye, Jasmine,' Mum shouted.

Opening the door, I went down a few steps and called out, 'Bye. See you soon girls. Don't worry – it won't be long.' and darted up the stairs again.

Alone in my room again, I plugged in my cassette and selected the backing tape that I used to help me make up lyrics. Headphones on, notepad in hand, I switched it on.

The beat took over. It wasn't long before words started to form in my mind and I began to write:

2

If you're feeling down
And you wanna get up
Just don't sit around and say
It's bad luck —
Cos this is life
You've got to be where it's at
So c'mon everybody
Just stand and clap

Say
I've got it
You've got it
We've all got it — it's life.
Yeah
I've got it
You've got it
We've all got it — it's life.

I kept saying it over and over again. It made me feel a bit better.

Mum popped her head round the door. 'You all right?'

I switched off the cassette. Shrugging my shoulders I said, 'I suppose so. Even if I wasn't, it doesn't matter.'

'Jasmine, there is nothing I can do. Even if I could afford to send you all over to your father in the States, he still couldn't look after you because of his studying. It just seems a waste of time to wait until he comes back home before I have my operation. Now when he does come back I'll be fit and well and ready to face the world.'

She tried to smile. It made me cry.

'Oh Mum,' I wailed. I felt really silly, but I couldn't help myself.

'Come on, Jasmine, don't cry honey. It'll only be for three, maybe four months at the most.'

'That's a long time, and you might even miss my sixteenth birthday. I could look after Rosa and Donelle, no problem

– anyway, I've looked after them all this half term – but you don't trust me.'

Mum sat on my bed. I took my headphones off.

'Jasmine, this is the last time I'm going to tell you. Brenda, my social worker, said that because you weren't sixteen, legally you had to go in a home, so there was no way you could've looked after the little ones. I know that you can, you know that you can, but they don't and it's the law of the land. It's a weight off my mind that Aunt Merri has agreed to have the two youngest –'

'Yeah, I'm glad I didn't have to go and stay with her. She may be Merri by name but that certainly isn't her nature – she's so miserable.'

'Okay, Jasmine, that's enough. Anyway, I'm glad too, that you won't be going into a home after all but staying with a foster family –'

'I'd rather go in a home. We don't even know a thing about this family – they could be a bunch of perverts for all we know and –'

'That's it, Jasmine.' Mum pointed her finger at me – it was a warning. 'Don't you let your mouth run away with you and step out of line, okay? One minute you don't want to go in a home, and after you've seen the home you want a foster family and now you've got that you're complaining.'

'But Mum, we haven't even seen the family yet.'

'Jasmine, you're wearing me out. Just make sure you've got everything you want packed and ready to leave later on.'

Mum got up slowly and went out. I felt guilty.

Lying on my bed I thought back to the time when I was first aware that Mum was ill. To me she was the strongest woman alive. She looked strong, big-boned, but not fat. Her hair was thick and jet black, as was her skin, which had a polished finish that made her look stronger still. Her eyes were the kind that seemed to know everything.

When Dad had been accepted to study marine biology in the University of Massachusetts, Mum encouraged him one hundred per cent. We saw him during the holidays, when

4

he came back to us in London — it was cheaper than all of us going to America. He had a year left. I wished he was here now.

I can't remember when Mum had started to complain of feeling tired. I didn't notice any change in her; illness and my mother just didn't seem to go together. Mind you I did notice that her stomach had started to look enormous.

'Mum, your stomach!' I'd tried to say tactfully.

'It's that time of the month, Jasmine.'

'What time of the month?' asked Rosa.

'It's women's business,' I said, feeling proud that I could answer her so.

'You're not a woman, Jas.'

Mum had laughed. 'She is Rosa, and you will be too, one day.'

I grinned. I liked Mum saying that.

Coming home from school one day, I found Mum at home; she had been sent home from work. It frightened the life out of me.

'What's wrong, Mum?'

It was then that she told me she had to go into hospital. 'The doctors say that they think I've got fibroids, and they feel it's best if they operate and see what needs to be done.'

I thought about what she had said.

'Well, it will only be for a couple of weeks, won't it, Mum?'

'No Jasmine, months. Maybe three or four. I have to have a time of convalescence too!'

That conversation seemed light years away now. It was in truth only seven months.

Now the time for the operation had come and I didn't want to face it. That was the trouble: I had pushed it out of my mind and hadn't really given it much thought.

My two friends Lisa and BB and I had just formed a girls' rapping group called 'BB.L. Jas Crew', and the raps we had composed were wicked. We had performed three times in all and had received mega-support from all our friends. I could feel that the three of us would be going places.

And now this.

I was going to be fostered out, but I would still be going to the same school. It wouldn't be the same, though. Mum was having an operation, Dad was in the States and Donelle and Rosa would be with Auntie Merri. The whole family would be mashed up, and just at a crucial time.

The thing that was killing me the most was Mum's operation. I had closed my mind to any thought of it going wrong. Somehow I believed that it would be all right, but − and it was a big but − what if something did go wrong? I sat up.

I wondered if I should pray, but I wasn't sure how you went about it. Mum was always making references to God, especially in the last couple of months, but what could I say to Him?

'Er, God − er, dear God, could you please look after Mum?' It sounded dry, even to me. I stood up and stretched.

I forced myself to stop worrying about Mum and think about this foster family. Brenda, Mum's social worker, seemed pretty cool. I didn't trust her though, after all the things you heard about social workers in the news. I hoped that she didn't think that Mum wasn't fit to be a mother and stop me from coming back home. I'd just simply run away. Anyway I was nearly sixteen: I could get married if I wanted to.

I had to admit that it had been Brenda's manoeuvrings and effort that had got me off the hook of going to the home. I had visited the home and it was awful. The place had a hospital smell and the kids looked wild.

'No way, Brenda, am I staying here. The kids look crazy and the staff look like rejects from a lunatic asylum.'

Brenda had laughed. 'Don't be like that, Jas. You'll get used to it after a while.'

I was adamant. 'No way. I'm not staying. Please find me somewhere else, or I don't know what I'd end up doing.'

It was blackmail, I know, but it worked.

Two weeks later Brenda had said that a fam[...]
Fentons would foster me. They wouldn't be able to me[...]
me as they had just gone on holiday, but would be back
in time to have me. And that was that.

I was a bit apprehensive. I wished now that I had been
able to meet them before. It was all such a hassle.

It was now five past six on a Friday night. Rosa and Donelle
had been gone three hours already and I should have left
five minutes ago.

'It's bad, isn't it Mum? What an impression to make,
being late like this. It's bad enough that Brenda couldn't
be here to introduce us.'

'It doesn't matter about introductions, and five minutes
isn't anything.'

I looked around the hall from my position on the stairs.
'Last time I'll be seeing you for ages.'

'Who you talking to, Jasmine?' Mum called from the
kitchen.

'The walls,' I replied.

'No need to be cheeky, girl.'

'Sorry Mum.'

'Anyway, I hope you'll be visiting me in hospital.'

The doorbell rang.

'I'll get it.' I stopped at the bottom of the stairs and
took a couple of deep breaths. Here goes, I said to myself
and with a smile plastered across my face swung open the
door.

'Hello. You must be Jasmine. I'm Mrs Fenton, but you
can call me Judy.' She held out her hand.

She was white. I froze.

Mum came up behind me. 'Hello, Mrs Fenton. I'm
Hilary, Jasmine's mum. Come in.'

I was speechless. With all my thoughts, and the
conversations I had had with my friends, about what my
foster family were going to be like, it had never occurred
to me that they might be white.

7

ually called the

..s Fenton was white, Mrs
..n to notice that we were black.
The prospect of leaving Mum was
..nd I didn't have time to talk to her about
..lopment.
..kissed and hugged and off I went with Judy.

Judy chatted all the way from my house to where she lived, which was about fifteen miles away. I answered her questions mechanically, my mind in confusion. How could Brenda foster me out to a white family? I just couldn't believe it.

Judy was now asking me if I was all right.

'Yeah.' I turned and looked out of the window. Why doesn't she shut up? Can't she see that I don't want to talk to her? I thought.

Evidently not: 'On Saturday we're having friends from church round for tea.'

'Church?' I couldn't help myself, it just came out.

'Yes,' she smiled, 'church. My family and I are regular churchgoers.'

'Well, excuse me, lady. I don't think I'll be going.'

'That's okay. Whatever you want to do.'

I was a bit disconcerted by that; I had expected her to try and force me. Still, I knew that I definitely wouldn't be going. I could use the time to write some more raps.

At last we were there. We pulled up outside quite a large house. I was impressed, but I was careful not to show it. Must have a bit of dosh, I thought.

'Oh, Aubrey must be home,' Judy said.

'Aubrey – what kind of a name is that?'

'It's my husband,' Judy replied with a grin. Nothing seemed to upset her; she could always find something to grin or smile about. I wondered if she was 'all there'.

I took my cassette recorder and left Judy to carry my two suitcases. She was struggling. Tough, I thought. She wanted me to be here. Let her and her family sweat.

Judy put the suitcases down and called out as she opened the door: 'Aubrey, Aubrey.'

I wanted to laugh. I was trying to guess what her husband looked like. She'd said he was an engineer. Probably half-bald with thick glasses; skinny, pale and anaemic-looking. I bet she has him right under her thumb, I thought. She wasn't bad looking: fair shoulder-length hair, a tan from the holiday and piercing blue eyes that didn't miss a trick, I would guess. She was about average height and I could see that she kept herself trim: probably an aerobics freak.

'Oh, there you are, love.'

I was stunned and nearly dropped my cassette — Aubrey caught it in time.

'You okay, Jasmine? You look as though you've seen a ghost.' He was a grinner too.

I might just as well have seen a ghost. Aubrey was black. This was really too much for one day, even for me.

2

'Tea or coffee, Jas? Or do you prefer something more
healthy — milk?' Judy offered.

I shrugged.

She smiled at me. 'Which one?'

'Milk, I suppose. Unless you have something stronger?'
I waited for an answer.

'Sure, if you want something stronger you can have sugar
in it.'

Aubrey burst out laughing. 'My wife is quick off the
mark.'

I grunted.

I looked around the room, careful to maintain my bored
expression, not that I'm particularly interested in kitchens.
This one could have come straight out of a magazine. It was
pine wood and white with every mod-con: dish-washer,
fridge-freezer with pine door, spotlights in the ceiling —
money obviously wasn't spared.

Judy was chatting away fifteen to the dozen, not noticing
whether or not I was listening. Aubrey was standing with
his back to me, fiddling about with some electrical
equipment.

Sitting at the long pine table, I was able to take them both
in. Aubrey was built like an athlete: tall (he must have been
six foot and over) with broad shoulders and long fingers that
looked clumsy but were not — he handled the tricky little
bits of wiring easily. Judy reached his shoulder, in height.
Without her tan she must have been quite fair and he was

quite dark. I wondered why he had married her. They looked like chalk and cheese. It was on the tip of my tongue to ask him.

Surely there must be hundreds if not thousands of beautiful black women he could have married. I thought of the magazines, *Ebony* and *Roots*, full to the brim of stunning women. If he didn't fancy any of those, there were black women all over London, England, the world! But he preferred a blondie. Madness! That put me off him.

'Jas, do you want a biscuit or a bun? A sandwich, perhaps?' Judy was looking at me.

I glared back. I didn't like way that she used my name so familiarly, as though we were great friends and had known one another for years.

'You okay, Jas? You don't mind us calling you Jas, do you?'

I lowered my eyes. 'No, it's okay,' I whispered.

Judy pulled out a chair and sat next to me. I could feel Aubrey's eyes on me. She touched my hands. 'I know it must be daunting for you to be plunged into the deep end of things and be expected to fit into a "strange" family, although as you get to know us, you'll realise that we're all right. Then of course you're probably worried about your mother. She'll be fine, we'll be praying for her and I'm confident that God will bring her through. You can visit her every evening if you want to.'

All of a sudden I felt like crying. I wasn't sure if it was the soft tones Judy was using (I suppose she was trying to get it across to me that she cared!) or the mentioning of my mum — anyway, traitor tears spilled down my cheeks. I pinched myself and squeezed my toes tightly to try to stop them. It was no use. They got worse. Fast and furious they flowed, like the rains in a Caribbean hurricane.

Judy hugged me tightly. Aubrey handed me some kitchen roll.

'There, there, you cry. It'll make you feel better,' Judy whispered.

11

This is not how I wanted things to be, I thought. The best thing would be to keep my mouth shut. So I did. I'd have to reason out why I had cried on my own later. Had I never done that before? Hmm.

I had started drinking my milk, which I must confess was quite refreshing, when the front door crashed open and banged closed. It sounded as if someone was demolishing it.

'Hi Mum. Hey Dad, what are you doing?'

'Matt, come on, have some manners, we have a guest,' Aubrey said nodding his head towards me.

'Oh, sorry. Hi. You must be Jas. Great name. Do you like jazz music by any chance?' He grinned.

'Do you like matt vinyl paint?' I said sarcastically.

Judy and Aubrey burst out laughing.

'That's great, Jas, hit him where it hurts,' Aubrey said, looking at Matt.

Matt did look hurt, but I'm sick of people saying 'Do you like jazz?' after hearing my name.

'Okay okay, first round to you. I'll think of something, don't you worry,' he said.

I felt a bit better.

'Want a drink Matt? You'll get your tea soon.'

'Thanks Mum, I'll have a glass of Coke.'

Judy didn't answer.

Aubrey did. 'What was that, son?'

Matt muttered under his breath, 'Some orange juice, please, Mum.'

'Okay, love,' Judy answered.

I wondered what that was all about.

Watching Matt drink his orange I became fascinated by his eyes. They were large, with ten-inch-long lashes that just curled up at the end, but what struck me most was the fact that they were grey! It seemed so strange, yet against his milky-coffee-coloured skin they were a nice contrast. His soft brown curly hair was cropped with a small 'tail' at the back. I could see that given a few more years to add to his thirteen he'd have the girls banging on his door!

12

'Are you a Christian, Jas?' Matt looked at me enquiringly.

'What do you mean?'

'Well, are you or aren't —'

Aubrey and Judy spoke together.

'Matt.'

'Matt.'

'Yes Mum, Dad?' Matt had a question-mark stamped across his forehead.

Aubrey looked annoyed, and Judy — well, I couldn't quite make out what the expression on her face was. It was Judy who answered.

'You don't need to ask Jas that question, or any other, for that matter. She's a guest in our house which doesn't mean that she must be subjected to a thousand and one personal questions, does it now?'

'But Mum —

'Did you hear me, Matt?'

'Matt, just finish your drink and go to your room. I'm sure you have some homework to do.' Aubrey spoke quietly, but I could sense the threat behind the words, even if Matt couldn't.

'Dad I — '

'Now.'

Matt gulped down his drink and made a hasty retreat out of the door.

'Take no notice of Matt, love. He's at an inquisitive age. Now, would you like to see your room? You'll be sharing with Cana, okay?'

I nodded.

Following Judy up the stairs I wondered what it would be like living with this family, and sharing a room with Cana. At home I had my own room, and I only let my sisters in when I wanted to. I love my own company. Being a private person, I shuddered at the thought of living at such close quarters with someone, and a stranger at that, for a few months.

Judy broke into my thoughts as we reached the bedroom

door. 'You'll enjoy sharing a room with Cana. She's great fun. It'll be like having a sister of nearly the same age — she's only about eighteen months older than you.'

Words failed me. I just looked at her but I wanted to ask how she could just assume that I wanted to have a sister of the same age, and how she knew that Cana's fun was my idea of fun.

As I stepped into the room, I could see straight away that my questions were answered. I know you can't tell a book by its cover, but judging by the decor of this room Cana and I were like two sides of a pound coin — different. Judy said that she would leave me to unpack and settle myself, after showing me which drawers and what part of the wardrobe were mine.

'Come downstairs when you've finished sorting out your things. Tea will probably be ready by then. Do you like rice?' She smiled.

I nodded, anything to get rid of her. Then, sort of smiling back (even that was an effort), I said, 'Okay.'

She closed the door. Peace at last.

Flopping down on the bed, I stared at the ceiling. I felt like crying again. I knew why that was — I was feeling so homesick. I missed Donelle and Rosa more than I thought I would, and as for Mum, well, just thinking of her name brought a lump to my throat.

I didn't want to unpack, I would gladly have picked up my suitcases and run out of the house all the way home. It was such a tempting thought, I could feel ideas beginning to churn around in my head.

'They don't really want you here Jas,' said a voice very loudly. I strained my ears to hear more. 'Just pick up your things and go. They can't stop you.'

Speaking quietly I said, 'But the social worker said that I couldn't live on my own as I was under age.' The voice said, 'Hah! What do social workers know? They're all for keeping families together regardless of circumstances.'

I knew that to be true. It was always in the newspapers

14

how social workers let children stay with their parents who were ill-treating them.

'But if I left here, they would put me in a home.'

'No, they won't.'

I sat up feeling very strange having this weird conversation. I got off the bed and began to unpack. I knew no matter what I said or thought I would have to stay here until Mum came out of hospital.

So shut up and get on with it, Jas, I said to myself.

Cana's room was quite big. It had pastel pink and white paintwork with silky wallpaper of the same colouring. There were furry cuddly toys all over the place. The windows were long with a ledge running around the bottom with a long cushion on it. At least it'll be comfortable to sit and look out of the window, I thought.

The wardrobe was built-in with white louvre doors. Cana's side was full of clothes and shoe boxes. Her parents must spoil her, I decided.

There were a lot of posters on the wall, some of artists I hadn't heard of before, like Amy Grant and Martyn Joseph. U2 I did know of, but they were *all* white.

A small stereo unit stood in the corner with a large cassette case and some LPs beside it. I had a quick look. Philip Bailey, now that's more like it, I thought. I wonder why she hasn't got him on the wall. Hmm. BeBe and CeCe Winan. Never heard of them, but at least they're black.

I had a look at her book selection on the shelf, too. Most of the titles I had never heard of before: *The Sacred Diary of Adrian Plass*, looks funny, *The Screwtape Letters* – hmm, C.S. Lewis? I thought for a moment. The name rang a bell, but I didn't know why.

Back to unpacking. My most important possession was my cassette. Just because I wasn't at home, there was no way I wasn't going to continue writing rap. That reminded me, I must phone Lisa and BB to sort out doing some more gigs.

As I pushed my suitcases under the bed, I felt a little

better, but I didn't want to go downstairs. I wasn't frightened or anything like that but, if the truth be known, I felt uncomfortable. I lay down on the bed, propped up by the pillows, with headphones on, getting in the mood to do some composing.

The door burst open and my heart gave a big 'thump' — I nearly leapt out of my skin.

'Hi Jas,' beamed this tall, slim, beautiful girl at me.

I just stared at her.

'I see you've settled in okay.' She came and sat at the end of my bed, still smiling.

I took my headphones off. 'Yeah.'

'What are you listening to?'

'Hmm, nothing in particular.'

'Let's have a listen.' She held out her hand. Something inside me didn't want her to listen, which was stupid, but I handed them over all the same.

Just before she put them on she said, 'I'm Cana.' Soon she was nodding her head and clicking her fingers. After a while she took the headphones off.

'Nothing but a beat really,' I said apologetically.

'No, it's great. I love heavy beats. Anyway, how are you? Feeling homesick? If I was in your position I'd be screaming and bawling if I had to stay with people I don't even know.' She grinned.

I didn't know whether I was going to like her or not. She had a lot of her mother in her, chatty and forward, yet like her mother she had something else that made you like her, in spite of yourself.

Summoning a grin of my own, I explained that I wrote rap music against the beat of the cassette.

'What!' she shouted excitedly. 'You write rap? That's mega.'

Her response really cheered me up. 'Yeah, I'm in a group.'

'No-o, really?' Cana boomed. 'What's it called?'

'The BB.L. Jas Crew. We've done three gigs already and we're looking out for a fourth.' I felt good telling her.

16

Cana jumped up, clapping her hands. 'This is wild. Wait till I tell my friends — they're going to be so jealous. Hey listen, can we come to your next gig?'

My eyes lit up. There's one way to get on my good side and that's to be interested in what I do. 'Cana, no problem. I'll even get you a complimentary ticket.'

She hugged me. 'Fan-tas-tic, Jas. I'm so glad you're staying with us.'

I thought that the hugging bit was over the top, but I let it pass — there wasn't much else I could do. But her saying she was glad I was here, and I think she meant it too, made me feel warm all over. 'I'm glad too,' I said.

Judy's voice cut through the door, almost piercing my ear-drums. 'Tea's up, girls.' Cana shouted back: 'Coming.'

That reinforced the massive vibrations ringing in my head. Going through the door I asked Cana why everyone shouted at each other.

'Family trait!' She laughed.

As I closed the door behind me I decided I would have to invest in some cotton wool.

I scraped my spoon around the bowl to make sure that I didn't leave behind any strawberry fool. I hadn't realised I was so hungry.

'Nice meal, Mum,' Matt said. 'Any more dessert?'

'No, but you can have some fruit.'

Matt sighed. 'That's boring.'

Aubrey spoke up. 'How can what God produces be boring?' He turned to me. 'In this house, Jas, we stay clear of junk food and anything that's harmful to the environment. Hence no fizzy drinks.' He flung a meaningful look at Matt who had made a face.

I'll have to drink my Coke or lemonade at school, or anyway out of the house, I told myself quickly.

Finding myself offering to do the washing up, to which Judy at first said no, and then insisting and going to the

17

sink to get on with it, I wondered if I was going mad. I hated washing up.

As I rinsed the dishes I was struck by how much my attitude had changed in such a short time. It was only a couple of hours since I'd arrived, unhappy and determined not to co-operate with this black and white mixture of a family. And yet here I was now, feeling full and comfortable and making a willing contribution. Even when everyone had closed their eyes and bent their heads over their plates as Aubrey prayed I had followed suit, though not without an inward groan.

I was discovering things about myself that only highlighted how much more I had to learn!

3

The spring sun flowed brightly through the floral curtains. I yawned and stretched myself the length of the bed. I could hear the birds tweeting to each other outside. It was nice to hear first thing in the morning. I wonder if I could work out a bird rap, I joked to myself.

I felt very comfortable in this room, surprisingly because I found it unsettling to sleep in a strange bed. I remembered the time I'd spent the night at BB's house. We had a great laugh and didn't get to sleep until the early hours of the morning, but when I woke up I felt lost for a couple of minutes until my brain registered where I was.

Looking across the room to see if Cana was still asleep I got a shock: she wasn't even in bed!

'Cana,' I called out, which was stupid as I could see that she wasn't in the room let alone the bed. I must be thick. Where could she be? The digital clock on her bedside table said 7.15.

It would be impossible for me to get used to getting up at this hour, especially on a Saturday when there wasn't any school.

Perhaps she was in the bathroom. In that case, I could stay in my snug bed, for a while at least. But what if she wasn't? I decided I'd better find out. If Cana was in the bathroom I would come back to bed. If she wasn't I would go downstairs and see if the rest of the family were up. And if they were, I would just have to get washed and dressed.

As soon as I opened the door I was hit by singing voices.

Wondering what was going on I walked gingerly to the bathroom and knocked on the door, calling Cana's name. No answer. Well, there was nobody in there.

At the top of the stairs the singing came over loud and clear. At first I thought it must be *Songs of Praise* on the telly. But that's in the evening, and anyway today was Saturday. What was going on?

Tiptoeing down the stairs I could tell the singing was coming from the front room. So it must be the family. It was a relief to know what was happening, and also that they hadn't tried to encourage me to join in. But to be honest, I felt a little left out. I had really been made to feel welcome yesterday and now this. Cana could have at least asked if I wanted to be included. Mind you, if Matt had had his way I'm sure he would have dragged me in by my hair, without bothering to ask!

I stood outside the front-room door trying to make up my mind — what should I do? Should I knock and go in or do something else — like go back to bed, for instance? I must admit that did seem like a good idea.

I was still dithering when the door whipped open and out walked Matt, colliding with me.

'Ouch! What are you standing here for?' he asked.

'Waiting for a bus.'

'Well you won't catch one here. Come in.'

He opened the door wider to let me through. I hesitated. Aubrey came to the door.

'Good morning, Jas. Sleep all right?'

I nodded.

'We're having family devotions. Would you like to join us?'

'I er, well I . . . '

'Well make your mind up. Yes or no?' Matt burst out.

Aubrey glared at him. 'Upstairs you.'

Matt shrugged his shoulders. 'Your loss, Jas. You don't know what you're missing,' he muttered.

'That's enough now, son,' Aubrey called after him.

Cana came to the door. 'Morning Jas. Did you sleep all right?'

'Fine.'

We stood in silence for what seemed an hour. Then we all spoke at once.

'Why don't you make yourself a cup of tea, Jas?'

'You can go back to bed if you like. I'll join you soon.'

'I'll come in.'

That seemed to settle it. Aubrey held out his arm and I calmly walked in.

Judy was sitting in one of the armchairs, with a book open on her lap. 'Good morning, Jas. Sleep okay?'

'Great.' I smiled at her — what else could I do?

'Sit next to me, Jas.' Cana pointed out a space next to an open book lying on the settee.

I sat down, waiting for something to happen.

Aubrey explained: 'Every Saturday and Sunday we all get together and have our own little family service. We read some Scriptures and sing some songs and pray. That's basically what happens. It's only an hour or so, depending on how many questions Matt decides to ask. We should be finished soon.' He smiled at me.

Judy piped up. 'It would be nice if you joined in, but please don't feel that you have to, just because you're staying with us. You can have a lie in.'

I didn't trust her. It seemed like a subtle way of saying: 'While you're with us — join in.' 'Hmm' was all I could muster up as an answer.

The door breezed open and in rushed Matt. 'Right, you've come in then. Good. We'll make a good Christian of you yet.'

Everyone spoke at once.

'That's enough, Matt.' Judy was being firm.

'I think we need to talk, son.' Aubrey spoke slowly and quietly, and a telling off was what he meant.

'Matt, you need to learn some manners.' This was in Cana's superior, big-sisterly voice. To me, she added. 'Take no notice, Jas,' with a whispered, 'little creep' that only I could hear.

I agreed.

What's the big thing about becoming a Christian? I wanted to ask. Matt kept dropping large hints about my not being one. Cana, I had to admit, hadn't even mentioned the fact. But even though Judy hadn't said anything obvious like Matt, I felt that underneath that cool exterior her brain was ticking away trying to suss out a way to steer me into becoming one. I would have to watch her. She never spoke straight. Her sentences were laced with hidden meanings.

Leaning back in the settee, I listened to what Aubrey was saying.

' . . . so healing comes about by believing and having faith − '

'But Dad, look at old Mrs Janson, she's always sick. Why doesn't Jesus heal her?'

'I honestly don't know son, but it's a good question. Why are some people healed and others not? It must be the will of God in an individual's life.'

Matt again. He was beginning to get on my nerves. 'But the Bible says that whatever we ask from God, we will receive, so − '

'Matt, why do you always have to be so difficult, eh?' Cana asked.

I wanted to second that. He was a typical little brother. In other words, a pain in the neck. I was glad that I didn't have a younger brother; bad as Donelle and Rosa were, I'm sure a brother would have been worse. Anyway, I would have had him under manners!

Boredom had begun to set in. I began to pass the time by examining my surroundings. The room was quite big. Large windows, heavy beige curtains, no nets. The walls were papered plain, with a few scenic pictures. The suite was like a chesterfield but covered with a floral material. There was a marble-like coffee table in the middle with a shelf underneath with some magazines on. The carpet was also beige, and thick. A bookcase, jam-packed with books, lined the whole of one wall. In fact I thought the room was rather bare. It was a bit like a doctor's or dentist's waiting room: nothing to take your mind off the impending pain!

' . . . but Dad, why do you have to go to see a doctor when Jesus, if you believe, can heal you?'

Aubrey sighed. 'Because, Matt, that may be how Jesus will heal you.'

'But Dad . . . '

I switched off again. I could see that before my time was up (and it seemed like 'doing time' with Matt around), the way he was getting under my skin, I'd probably have to slap him about, get some sense into his head. He must be going through that difficult stage of adolescence that makes some people go mad. Funnily enough I couldn't remember being anything remotely like him at his age. Little horror.

There was nothing more to study in the room so I began to scrutinise the rest of the family. Aubrey was handsome and reminded me of my dad (I must get a letter in the post to him as soon as possible), but he was taller and broader. His skin was like dark oak and so were his eyes, large and soulful. I could see where Matt got the shape of his, if not that amazing colour. He did give you that feeling of strength and dependability. I wondered if that was one of the reasons Judy married him. I still couldn't understand *his* marrying Judy. I studied her, trying to reason out why, yet not finding an answer. Blonde, blue-eyed, small facial features, full stop. There must've been something, perhaps she wooed him! Mum was always saying that that's how some women got their men. I suppose that's what they call 'womanly wiles'. There was more to Judy than the eye could see.

Next Cana. She could easily have been a model. When I first saw her zoom into the room, it was her height and her hair that took my breath away. She looked like an Amazon. She seemed about seven foot tall and her hair, a shoulder-length mass of curls, was flying all over the place. I could see that boys would fancy her. She was definitely a mixture of her mother and father: her skin the colour of nutmeg, her eyes smallish (and green!), tall and slim. A nice combination.

'Jas, Jas.'

I looked up, my brain struggling to focus on whose voice was calling my name.

'Jas. You okay?'

'Yeah,' I said dreamily. It was Judy; I might've guessed.

'We're going to pray now. Is there anything you want us to pray about?'

'No.' I stared at her as though she was mad, which she could well be. Fancy asking me a question like that!

'What about your mum?'

'Yeah, what about her?' She wanted me to cry again, I could sense it.

'Well, she is in hospital and I wondered if you would like us to pray that Jesus will help her.'

'Okay, if you want.'

I had a sudden urge to jump up and run out of the room. But I dug my fingernails into my legs to stop myself.

Everybody was looking at me and smiling. I tried to grin back.

This family was a bunch of nutters, just how I would imagine a group of lunatics to be: smiling all the while, when there was nothing to smile at, trying to transfer their madness on to you.

'Let's pray,' said Aubrey. They all kneeled down.

That's it, I thought. I'm going to see Brenda on Monday to ask her to find me somewhere else. They are all a hundred per cent fruitcakes. Kneeling on the floor. Crackpots! Wait till I tell Mum. She'll go mad and want me to leave instantly. I felt sick.

As I sat there on the settee (I saw no reason to kneel, so I didn't) my mind was a jumble of thoughts, the main one being how to get away. It would take some planning to convince my social worker that I just couldn't stay — but the fact of the matter was I just could stay.

24

'Amen,' Aubrey said.

In about two seconds it was as if I had imagined the whole thing. Matt was up and out of the door, followed by Aubrey. Judy was asking what I wanted for breakfast, and Cana was inviting me to go shopping with her and then on to see her great-aunt. 'We won't stay long, as I'll have to help Mum get things ready for tea.' I just said yes to shut everybody up.

Over breakfast Judy asked when I wanted to see my mum.

'Eh, probably tomorrow,' I said. That would get me out of going to church. Good move, I thought.

'That would be great. You can go after church. We'll take you.'

She must've seen the shocked look on my face, because she added quickly, 'That's if you want us to come.'

'Well, eh, I don't mind.'

'Okay then, Jas. After church we'll all go and see your mum. That's settled then.'

I wanted to say that that wasn't the issue, neither was anything settled. Who said I wanted to go to church in the first place? I could see quite clearly that when Judy wanted something, she made sure she got it. That put the seal on the idea that poor old Aubrey didn't have a leg to stand on when he met her. She wanted him and she obviously didn't stop until she got him!

Well, she may have won this round, but I'm going to play her at her own game, I decided. I won't contact Brenda, I'm going to stay and fight this woman who manipulates people, especially black men (well, man — her husband in fact). She's certainly met her match in me. Christian or not, I'll take her on.

Instantly into my mind popped the title of a rap I could write about Judy: 'Don't let the power take you over.' That was her right on the button.

I must find out more about her, I thought. I'll probe Cana on the way to her great-aunt's.

4

'Two cauliflowers for just fifty pence, c'mon girls, bargain of the day.'

'Cucumbers twenty pee, twenty pee.'

Walking through Romford Market with Cana was like being let out of prison after serving ten years. There was so much activity — everything was alive.

'This fresh air is great.'

'Yeah, it's a nice morning,' said Cana.

'You know, it seems strange living with another family. Even though it's only been a night and a morning, I felt caged in.'

Cana laughed. 'You mean my mum.' She saw me hesitate.

'Well . . . '

'You don't have to explain. Mum's like that. She's really a very considerate person, but she does like to have things, and people, in order.'

'Hmm, so I've noticed.'

Waiting at the shoe stall while Cana tried on what seemed like every pair, I heard someone calling my name. It was Lisa.

'Jas, Jas. What's happening, girl?'

'Hi Lisa.' I grinned at her.

We hugged as though we hadn't seen each other for a hundred years!

'I phoned you yesterday but your mum said that you had gone already and she couldn't remember where she had written down the number of where you are staying.'

'I would've seen you in school on Monday and you could've got it then.'

'Yeah, I know, but I thought staying with strangers you would've been pleased to have got a buzz from a friend, eh?'

'That was nice of you Lisa.'

Lisa smiled and shrugged. I think she felt a little embarrassed showing her concern for me. It's a good feeling to know that your friends do care.

Lisa is about two inches taller than me. She has her hair in single plaits with blonde bits in, and the ends are curly. Like me she wears a lot of jewellery. Big hoop ear-rings and lots of bangles on both arms, but I only wear three rings altogether on my fingers, while Lisa has a ring on each of hers! She had even pierced her nose — something my mum would never allow.

'Who are you with?' asked Lisa.

I pointed to Cana's back.

Lisa whispered, 'Who's she?'

I mouthed back, 'The family I'm staying with — their daughter.'

Lisa nodded.

At that moment Cana turned round. 'What do you think of these, Jas?' She was holding up a pair of purple suede shoes.

'Okay.'

'I think I might get them. What do you think?'

'They're all right.'

'Is that all you can say, all right?'

'Well, what do you want me to say?'

Lisa piped up, 'Yeah, you should get them.'

Cana looked in puzzlement at Lisa, as if to say 'Who's she?'

'My friend Lisa, a member of the group.' I knew that would jog her brain.

'Oh that Lisa, right.'

Lisa continued with her opinion: 'If you have a purple jacket, preferably suede, if not then whatever you've got,

27

baggy black trousers, short black top' — she made an 'O' shape with her finger and thumb — 'you'll look the business.'

Cana laughed. 'Do you think so?'

'Yeah, once I say something, you can put your money on it, all right?'

Opening up her bag, Cana took her purse out.

'You half-caste then?' Lisa asked her suddenly.

Cana's hand was poised in mid-air for a fraction of a second. 'Of mixed parentage? Yes, I am.'

'Oh, I thought so. You have the look.'

I was beginning to feel a little uncomfortable.

'Who's white, then, your mum or your dad?' Lisa ploughed on, oblivious.

Speaking gently Cana said, 'My mum.'

'Oh, I see.'

It was time to change the subject as I felt the conversation was getting hotter than the weather. 'When's the next rehearsal, Lisa?'

'Eh, Wednesday at the youth club.'

'Usual time?'

'Eh, yeah. Talking of time, I've got to run. My mum will kill me. I've been out since early morning and she wanted me to help her do something. So listen, see you Monday, Jas, and — sorry, I didn't catch your name.'

'Cana, I didn't introduce you both, did I?'

'No you didn't, Jas,' Lisa replied. 'But not to worry. See you again sometime, Cana, all right?' She turned and was gone, lost in the crowd.

Browsing through the market not looking at anything in particular, I could sense that Cana was a little upset. Obviously it was what Lisa had asked her about her parents. I didn't feel like going into it myself just then so I told her I wanted to phone my mum before she left home for the hospital.

The first phone box we came to required a phone card. I didn't have one, but Cana did. 'Here, borrow mine.'

28

'I'll pay you back later.'

'Don't worry, it's no big deal.'

'Thanks.'

The phone rang for ages. I was about to put it down when someone answered.

'Hello Mum . . . oh sorry, Aunt Lyn. Is my mum there? Thanks.'

Turning to Cana, I told her that I was just in time as Aunt Lyn, my mum's close friend, was just leaving with her for the hospital.

'Oh, hi Mum. Everything all right? . . . the family are nice . . . lovely food . . . nice house . . . I'm coming to see you tomorrow, yeah . . . After church, the family want to come too . . . You sure, Mum? . . . Okay . . . Give my love to Aunt Lyn . . . Bye . . . ' I replaced the receiver.

'How is she?' Cana enquired.

'She seems fine. She wouldn't let on anyway if she didn't feel too good.'

'Your mother doesn't want you to worry, that's why.'

'Yeah, I suppose so.'

We carried on walking in silence. Since I had left home I hadn't really thought about Mum. That's not strictly true. I didn't want to think about her going into hospital. Brenda had explained to me the operation that Mum would be having — apparently it was quite a major one. Dad had phoned from the States virtually every evening; he too was worried. He wanted to come home and look after us, but Mum wouldn't have it. They had had a terrible argument. If Mum hadn't pleaded with Dad so strongly he would have been on the first plane home!

I had promised to write to my Dad regularly on Mum's progress as well as Donelle's, Rosa's and mine. I would certainly have a lot to tell him about the Fentons.

'Quick, run. That's our bus,' Cana shouted.

Her voice was so loud, it nearly gave me a heart attack. But I still ran after her as though a monster was chasing me. We made it.

Breathlessly Cana said, 'You're quite a sprinter.'

I couldn't answer at first as I felt a bit dizzy. 'I, eh, I had no choice.'

Cana laughed. 'Anyway we caught the bus.'

It took half an hour to get to Ilford in which time Cana filled me in about her great-aunt. She was on Aubrey's side of the family. She had been partly responsible for bringing up Aubrey when he had lived in Jamaica. 'He's still very close to her. She's quite sweet really. When I was younger she used to frighten me a bit, but as I got older I could see that she's really quite harmless. Her name is Aunt Myrtle and she's a little deaf — but she seems to hear what she wants to, when it suits her. She's also a very strong Christian. Thinks women shouldn't wear trousers or make-up, and it's an abomination not to wear a hat to church.'

'A bomb what?'

'It just means something God doesn't like,' she said with a laugh.

I wondered how Judy got on with Aunt Myrtle. I asked Cana.

'Eh, quite well. They're both strong personalities.' She ended it there. I found what she *didn't* say more interesting. I wondered how Aunt Myrtle felt about Aubrey and Judy's marriage.

Once we got off the bus in Ilford High Road, the walk to Aunt Myrtle's house seemed to take longer than the bus ride.

'Couldn't we have got a bus?' I had seen two pass us as we'd been walking.

'Yeah we could've done, but it's such a nice day, and you did say that you liked the fresh air.'

I didn't answer her as what I would've said would definitely have wiped the little smile off her face. So much for Christianity! I was finding out that Cana (who has more of her mother than her father in her) could be every bit as 'difficult' as Matt.

By the time we stopped at a house with a well-kept front

garden, I was curious to find out more about Aunt Myrtle.

Cana rang the bell. No answer. Banging on the door knocker brought no results either.

'She must be in. I only spoke to her yesterday, she knew we were coming.'

I was just about to say 'So you had assumed *yesterday* that today was on, and that I was coming to your great-aunt's' when Cana whipped out a key from her pocket. At the same time the next-door neighbour came out — a middle-aged woman who must've just come from the hairdressers: her hair was well set, so was her mouth.

'Hello Cana,' said the woman.

'Hello Mrs Lipper. I can't seem to get any answer from Auntie.'

'Funny you should say that. As a rule on Friday evenings she knocks on the wall, which means if we're going to the Chinese she puts in an order too.' She folded her arms. 'Well, she didn't. So I said to my Ted, I wonder if Myrtle's all right, but he just said she's probably sleeping. I said I'd knock and wake her up and he said that I've got to remember that she's an old woman and it's best if I don't disturb her. So I didn't.' She nodded her head.

'That was stupid. She could be dead,' I blurted out before I realised that it was something that should have been left to my thoughts.

There was an uncomfortable silence.

'Thanks Mrs Lipper. I've got the key, I'll find out what's happened to Auntie.' Cana opened the door.

I didn't want to go in, but my legs had a will of their own. I followed her.

'Auntie, Auntie,' called Cana.

'Do you think she's all right?'

I didn't get a reply. That told me that what I had said had upset Cana, which was understandable, but it must've been on her mind too. I wanted all the more to turn tail and run. I followed Cana up the stairs.

We heard a noise.

31

The feeling I got was like when you are watching a horror film and the music is haunting and it slowly builds up in a crescendo and someone opens a cupboard door and a body falls out.

'Cana, what do you think has happened to Aunt Myrtle?'

Cana didn't speak. She couldn't still be annoyed with me. I was getting a bit fed up with the cold-shoulder treatment.

It was then we heard somebody say, 'Who's dere?'

'It's Aunt Myrtle.' Cana let out a sigh of relief. Pushing open the nearest door revealed Aunt Myrtle propped up on the floor. 'Oh, Aunt Myrtle. What's wrong?' Cana was nearly crying.

I stood by the door.

'Mi chile, who woulda ever believe it. Mi don't rightly know how it occur. All mi know sey is, mi push open de door and mi fall down. An mi try an try fi get up, nuttin doing. So mi know sey yu is coming today wid yur friend, so mi just make mi bed right here.' She pointed to the floor. Looking up at me she said, 'Dis yur friend, is why she have on so much gold, ee?'

This was a time when I wished I had an ear-ring in my nose! Cana didn't answer but asked: 'Auntie, are you in pain?'

'Yes mi chile, mi tink sey mi bruck mi foot, but mi know dat God will heal it, praise His name.'

'Listen Auntie. I'll have to call an ambulance and Dad and sort something out. Jas, you stay with Auntie while I make the phone calls.'

Cana was getting more and more like her mother by the minute. She didn't even ask me if I would like to wait with her, she just told me! I was left with the problem of what to say to an old woman. I was racking my brains to think of something that might interest her. I needn't have worried – she was full of it. I could see where Matt got it from.

'What is your name darlin?'

'Jas.'

'Who?' said Aunt Myrtle accusingly. I felt awful.

32

'Jasmine,' I said reluctantly.

'Jasmine. Dat is better. Where yur mudda?'

'In hospital.'

'Hmm, an so yu is staying with Aubrey, mi nephew.'

I noticed that she hadn't mentioned Judy's name. I brightened up a little bit. 'Yeah, that's right.'

'Yes. Mi did help fi rear him, yu know. Him turn out lovely. An, him still a serve de Lawd, praise His name. Yu know Jesus as yur personal Saviour chile?'

I gulped — this woman was lethal. 'I eh, I hmm, what do you mean?'

She pointed towards the dressing table. 'Pass mi eyeglass.'

The dressing table was covered with an assortment of things. I couldn't see them at first, but that didn't impress Aunt Myrtle.

'It look like yu need de eyeglass den. Yu can't find dem?'

Just as she said that I found them. 'Here they are.' I handed them to her proudly.

She snatched them. The force of the woman made me think that even though she might have broken some bones, she was still as strong as an ox.

'Now. Yu is a Christian?'

What could I say but 'No'?

'Don't worry yurself.'

I was about to tell her that I wasn't when she continued: 'De grace of God, praise His name, still abounds where dere is sin. So, nar worry, yur time is nigh. Surrender yur life now and receive full salvation, yu understand.'

I blinked. I didn't know whether she was a raving lunatic or the pain of her leg was having a bad effect on her brain. I wanted to laugh. Here was this little old woman (I must admit she wasn't particularly grey-haired), wearing bifocal glasses (obviously blind as a bat), defenceless, telling me to receive full salvation. I couldn't wait to tell Mum. Pity they were all coming to the hospital with me on Sunday — knowing Judy she probably wanted to make sure that I didn't say anything bad about them. But I would be seeing

33

Mum on her own some other time so that didn't matter. Aunt Myrtle, I thought, would've got on like a house on fire with Aunt Merri.

Cana came into the room. 'Aunt Myrtle, Dad's coming over now — I got him on his carphone. The ambulance is coming too.'

'Yu didn't need to call de ambulance, chile. Mi will be all right.'

'Aunt Myrtle,' Cana sighed. She sat on the floor next to her and put her arm around her neck. 'You might have to stay with us.'

'No, no, no. Mi want to stay right here in mi own house. Mi nar want to be a burden to nobody, yu understand.'

That statement added to my impression that Aunt Myrtle and Judy didn't see eye to eye. Well, we'd have to see.

The doorbell rang. Cana said it must be her dad. She was right.

Aubrey came straight into the room and began fussing over Aunt Myrtle so much he was beginning to get on my nerves. Aunt Myrtle wasn't too happy either.

'Cana, pack some things for Aunt Myrtle.'

'No, no, no. Mi going to stay in mi own house.'

'You just do what I say, Cana.'

The doorbell rang again.

'That'll be the ambulance,' announced Aubrey.

I wanted to give him ten out of ten for that bit of information. They were expected and we all knew that it couldn't have been anyone else.

The ambulancemen (it was actually a man and a woman) were very professional and before Aunt Myrtle knew it, she was trussed up like a turkey ready for baking and, under protest, she was carried downstairs. We followed the ambulance in Aubrey's Vauxhall estate.

The wait at the hospital wasn't long, which was surprising, and Aunt Myrtle was soon sitting upright in bed.

'Auntie,' said Aubrey, 'you're only here for a week at the most and then you'll be staying with us.'

34

Aunt Myrtle didn't agree, to put it mildly. She raised her voice and tried to get out of bed. I was so embarrassed. I was glad that I didn't know anyone in the ward — otherwise I would've died. Cana and her dad seemed so cool. They must have had a lot of practice. A dreadful thought came to my mind: Aunt Myrtle would be staying at the house while I was there. I didn't know whether I could stand it. The family, being Christian, were a bit peculiar to say the least. Judy was the strangest, followed by Matt and Cana, only Aubrey seeming sane — for now. If Aunt Myrtle's added to the family, I thought, I'll have to ask Brenda if another placement can be found for me. Under the pressures of my mum being in hospital and living with these religious fanatics, what will keep *me* from crossing that delicate line over to insanity?

There must be a way out.

5

'What a terrible thing to have happened to your aunt
Aubrey.' These words of concern were from Jean, a friend
of the family's, who also attended their church and had been
invited for tea.

'She's very stubborn and insists on doing her own thing.
It's a wonder she hasn't fallen down and broken something
long ago,' said Judy.

Funny how she can recognise stubbornness in somebody
else and not herself. But then, that's a common human
complaint. Never see your own faults or fail to see everyone
else's. Typical.

All the people that had been invited for tea had turned
up except Mrs Christodoulou and her son Aszal. If the lot
already here were anything to go by, they certainly weren't
going to be a bundle of fun. Ten people had come; six adults
and four teenagers. I would have preferred to stay with the
adults but being of an age when you aren't allowed to think
for yourself I had to comply.

We congregated in Cana's room. I sat on my bed, Cana
on hers, Matt and his friend Simon on the window-ledge,
Cana's friend Sara on the floor propped against Cana's bed,
and Martin and Christina (brother and sister) on the floor
by the stereo.

'So you're in a rap group. What do you do?' This bright
question came from Simon. I could have guessed that
nothing intelligent would come from anyone who had
something in common with Matt.

36

'What do you think a rap group does?' I couldn't help being sarcastic.

'Keep your shirt on. I suppose you rap.' He sniggered.

'No, we punch little boys' heads in.'

Matt and Simon burst out laughing. 'I told you she was wild.'

That got right up my nose, the thought that Matt had been discussing me. 'What else did Inspector Matt tell you about me?'

They both oohed and aahed.

'Well? I'm waiting.'

Cana piped up: 'Let's leave it boys, eh? Now then what shall we do?'

Trust Cana to smooth over the atmosphere, which left to me would have become violent. Suggestions for what to do flew all over the place. I didn't like the sound of any of them.

'If you'll excuse me I've got something I'd like to do, *alone*.' Before anyone could say a word I got off the bed and, picking up my cassette, pen and writing pad, left the room.

Standing outside the door, I felt fed up. To be truthful, writing rap was the last thing I wanted to do, but I just couldn't bear the thought of spending the afternoon playing silly games with them. They all seemed so childish. To be quite blunt, they made me sick.

Since I had been here (even though it was only a day and a night), I hadn't had any time to myself — to think, to breathe. Everyone lived on top of each other.

Opening the door of the spare room, I breathed a sigh of relief: This is more like it. The room was a reasonable size. There was an unmade bed with two pillows along one side of the wall. The windows didn't have any curtains up which made the room very bright.

I didn't think Aunt Myrtle would be able to get all her gear in there and I wondered whether Judy would give up her bedroom and stay in this one. Somehow I couldn't see that happening.

On the wall were three posters. One said: 'The wages of sin is death, but the gift of God is eternal life in Christ Jesus our Lord' (Rom. 6:23). It had a picture of a hill — all black but surrounded by a bright sunset.

The second said: 'For God so loved the world that he gave his one and only Son, that whoever believes in him shall not perish but have eternal life' (John 3:16). The picture was of a man holding a lamb like a baby, a shepherd, I supposed.

The last one said: 'Here I am! I stand at the door and knock. If anyone hears my voice and opens the door, I will come in and eat with him, and he with me' (Rev. 3:20), and showed a man standing outside a door knocking.

Funny posters, I thought. I reread them a few times and got the gist of them — become a Christian. Aloud, I said 'Big deal.' And was it such a big deal? I didn't think so!

After plugging in the cassette and sitting on the bed, I tried to figure out the difference between Cana, Matt, Judy and Aubrey and myself. We all ate the same food, we dressed similarly (well, nearly the same), we spoke the same language (again I wasn't too sure about that: sometimes I thought Judy spoke double-Dutch!). I couldn't think of anything about them that was miles apart from me, that said they were 'Christians' and I wasn't! Their behaviour certainly wasn't 'turn the other cheek'. Well, that's what my mum said Christians were supposed to do. Matt was a little sneak, Cana was touchy and Judy — I couldn't quite put into words what I felt about her, but given enough time, I was sure it would come. The only one that seemed okay was Aubrey, who was nice, but so are a lot of people who aren't Christians.

I wrote the title 'Don't let the power take you over' on the top of the page, put my headphones on and tuned in the cassette. Leaning against the wall, I let the beat of the music get into me so that I could feel it. I knew the words wouldn't be a long time coming.

But I sat for ages waiting for some words to form in my mind — nothing. I couldn't understand it. Was I losing my touch? There was no way that I could afford to, the group depended on me for the words.

I was a bit frightened and wondered if I had writer's block or whatever it's called. I lay down hoping it might relax me enough to write something. Nothing.

There was a niggling thought at the back of my mind about the cause of my brain block, but it seemed ridiculous. Okay, a strange house, a different room would put anyone off from being creative, but I was sure I could handle that. It had to be the posters. Especially the one about the door, that seemed a bit spooky. If I had been on my own territory and someone had shown them to me I probably would have shrugged my shoulders, not taken much notice, but somehow, here in this room, it was a little, well, unnerving.

I looked up at the wall and read each poster again. Not for anything could I understand why I just didn't feel right.

It's no good, I thought, I can't write anything in here. Taking off the headphones and switching the cassette off, I gave up the idea of writing anything.

I was stuck for something to do. I didn't want to go back to Cana and her idiot friends. I wasn't particularly welcome downstairs.

I decided on a nap, or rather I felt drowsy and was finding it hard to keep my eyes open. I was stretched out with my hands behind my head, nice and comfortable (Aunt Myrtle would be all right on this bed, I thought). I could feel my eyelids growing heavy and the motion of my chest going in and out soon had me in the Land of Nod.

I was sitting on a wooden stool in a room which was bare except for a golden box over by the door. I wasn't frightened; just puzzled. I didn't know where I was. I wasn't sure if it was really happening or if I was dreaming, it was so real!

There was only the one door and one little window, the size of a small loaf of bread, with no window-pane. I kept wondering where my mum and dad and Donelle and Rosa were. I looked over to the door and it suddenly dawned on me that there wasn't a keyhole or a door handle.

The words 'This is strange' kept going over and over in my mind. I was feeling hungry too. I walked over to the box and tried to pick it up. I couldn't. It was red hot. The funny thing was it didn't look hot, but it nearly burnt my fingers.

I sat back down on the stool and was blowing my singed fingers when the light in the room — wherever it came from, there was no bulb and the window couldn't let in enough light to brighten up a mousehole — dimmed.

'Come on. The game's over,' I called out, reasoning that someone must be having a joke on me. Then I remembered that I was staying with the Fentons. One of them must be playing tricks on me: Matt, I decided, thinking I had cracked the mystery.

'All right Matt, you've had your laugh, open the door and let me out.'

No answer.

There was no option but to bang on the door. I didn't want to because I didn't want Matt to think that he had scared me. So I hung on for a few seconds.

'Right. That's it. Open the door *now*!' I jumped up, made a rush for the door and began to bang on it with all the strength I could muster.

No response.

That's not quite true. There was a response: the light went out completely.

I was in total darkness. This was serious.

'Let me out this minute, Matt Fenton, and I won't do anything to you, but if you don't you'll be for it.' I was quite angry by now. To think that a stupid little schoolboy was holding me captive against my will, and was probably having a good laugh with his friends. That would make even the most peace-loving person violent.

'Open up, Matt.'

There I stood in the darkness, leaning against the door

— helpless. I couldn't break the window-pane — there wasn't one, and the window was too small even to look out and call for help, let alone climb out. The thing that was beginning to get to me was the silence. I had never realised that silence could give you brain damage: no one to talk to, not even a bird tweeting to stimulate your brain, just a deafening silence.

I wanted to go to the loo.

'What is happening?' My voice didn't even sound like my own.

Then a voice, which definitely wasn't mine, said: 'I want to talk to you.'

I gulped in a gallon of air. My throat was so dry my tongue felt as if it was going to crack. I opened my mouth to speak, but nothing came out.

'Jasmine?'

I couldn't answer.

'Listen carefully.'

My tongue came to life. 'No. You listen, you creep. Do you know what they do to men who hold women against their will?'

The voice didn't reply.

'Well, they, they, hmm, they put you in a cell on your own and, hmm, you only have bread and water to eat and. . .'

'Jasmine. Calm down.'

Buckets of sweat poured down my face, my heart was beating out a wicked rap and my knees had dissolved. This was it. I was going to die. There was one thought racing round in my head: *go down screaming*. Whoever was after me wasn't going to have it that easy. My mouth opened wide like a killer whale having his lunch and a sonic boom blasted out, its tail end being pushed out by my stomach muscles. It was a deafening sound.

'Jas, Jas, wake up. It's okay.'

My eyelids flashed open. The light in the room caused me to screw them up tightly. I could hear a lot of voices, people talking all at once.

'She okay?'

'Must've been a nightmare.'

'A nightmare at this time of the day? Needs her head seeing to, ha, ha.'

'Be quiet.'

I started whimpering and shivering at the same time.

'It's okay, Jas. You're all right now,' Aubrey said soothingly.

Being hugged tightly was very reassuring. After the experience I had gone through a drop of Mum's white rum would have brought me back to myself.

'A man was, was after me.' I couldn't believe it was my voice I was hearing.

'Everyone out.' I knew that voice − it was Judy.

With my eyes still closed (I didn't want to see anyone) I kept wondering what had happened. Then I heard a voice I didn't recognise say: 'Will she be all right now?'

Without waiting to hear the answer, I had to open my eyes. I couldn't help it. My heart felt as though it was beating the last few times before going into permanent retirement.

A pair of almond-shaped brown eyes with tiny green specks in them covered by round gold-rimmed glasses were piercing a hole into mine. Thick, black, arched eyebrows were creased into a frown. A few strands of curls were hanging over the left eye. The face was bright and glowing as though it had been scrubbed for hours. The soft olive complexion made me want to reach out and touch it. A dark line over the top lip which was quite thick and pink made me wonder if this was a boy or a man.

He smiled. I didn't do anything.

He straightened up and walked out of the door.

'You okay now, Jas?' I looked up at Cana. I hadn't even realised she was in the room. I nodded. She walked out.

That left me and Judy.

'Do you want to tell me about it?'

I didn't. But I did.

Her answer didn't enlighten me one bit. 'It may mean a

number of things, then again it may not mean anything. Remember you've only been with us a day or so and it's still all new.'

You can say that again.

'Once you get into the routine of things you'll be all right.' She kissed my cheek and gave me a squeeze. 'Okay?' she added with a smile.

I nodded.

Judy stood up and looked around the room. 'I don't know how Aunt Myrtle is going to fit her stuff in here. I asked Aubrey if we should move in here and give her our room. Hmm, something has to be worked out.' Turning back to me, she said: 'See you downstairs, Jas.'

It would be putting it mildly to say that I didn't feel myself. First I had a nightmare — or was it real? Then I had come face to face with some guy I had never seen before in my life, which had nearly given me a heart attack. Finally Judy springs a surprise on me by saying that she's thinking of giving up her bedroom to Aunt Myrtle.

This was all too much for me. I would have to have a word with Brenda on Monday, otherwise I didn't think I'd be able to last the few months here — physically!

6

'There's so much traffic on the road. Where is everyone going?' asked Cana.

I just couldn't resist it. 'To church.' The sarcasm was dripping off my tongue.

Trust Judy not to be affected. 'You're probably right Jas.'

That shut me up — for now.

The journey to church took nearly three-quarters of an hour. I couldn't see the point of going so far. Why not pick a nearer church?

Anyway, after the initial burst of conversation everyone appeared to be deep in their thoughts, or perhaps they had run out of things to say, which is unusual for this family. The silence gave me time to think back to yesterday evening.

I was not myself, to say the least. For a start the dream or nightmare or whatever it was was like something you might see on the programme *The Twilight Zone*. It seemed so real, yet it wasn't. I have never (as far as I can remember) ever experienced anything like it. No, that's not quite true: I do remember something that happened a few years back. It was when my dad first started studying abroad and Mum said it was associated with that fact. I had a kind of nightmare and was very restless and sweating like a rainy day, but I didn't wake up screaming my head off.

This recent episode was a whole new ball game. The frightening thing for me was that it had seemed as though it was actually taking place. The room, the stool, the golden box and the locked door without a handle — how could it be explained? I secretly thought it had something to do with the posters on the wall, but I just couldn't see a connection.

As if that wasn't enough on my plate I now had pictures of Aszal running round my brain, stirring up my grey matter. His was the face that was deeply printed on my mind, from the moment I woke up from the nightmare to going to sleep last night, and waking up this morning.

The way I felt about him (I don't fancy him or anything stupid like that, I told myself, he's certainly not my type) was just strange. I couldn't put it into words. That made it worse, not being able to reason it out in my mind.

Sitting downstairs with everyone yesterday evening I'd felt like a pop star surrounded by unwanted fans. Everyone had been fussing over me.

'Would you like something to eat, Jas?'

'Are you feeling all right?'

'Sure there's nothing you want?'

Yeah, I thought, for you to leave me alone. I sat in the corner, hoping to become invisible. Wishful thinking.

So there I was minding my own business when who should come and squat on the floor beside me? Aszal.

I must confess at this point, I didn't mind talking to him. I wondered what his name was.

He came out and told me. 'Hi. My name is Aszal. I guess you're Jas. Nice to meet you.'

Hazily I wondered how he knew my name. Hmm. I sort of smiled. I didn't know what else to do.

'It must've been quite a scare you had.'

'It was.'

'Listen, hmm, is there anything you want to talk about? I, hmm, I don't mean to pry. You can tell me to get lost or something.'

Under normal circumstances after the first few words I would have told him to push off, but I didn't. In fact I told him all about the nightmare.

45

He listened patiently. I was expecting him to tell me I was mad. He didn't.

'These things can happen to anyone.' He sat looking thoughtfully at me. 'I, hmm, would like to ask you something, but please don't take any offence — I really don't mean it.'

It was on the tip of my tongue to say 'Yes', but I thought I had better be cool, so I just shrugged.

'You sure?'

I wanted to shout out: 'Get on with it.' Instead I nodded.

'Well, I wanted to know if I could pray with you. I really feel that we should bring Jesus in on this.' He held up his hands when he saw my reaction. I was shocked at him saying such a thing. I had completely forgotten that this lot were from church.

But what was even more surprising to me was that I said yes.

I felt good after he prayed, mainly because his voice was crisp and precise, and it somehow had a calming effect on me.

I was so glad when everyone had gone home. Cana and I helped Judy to tidy up. No one (that is Judy) asked me how I felt, which was good as I wasn't in the mood to make polite conversation.

Sitting up in bed, Cana and I talked about the evening. I wanted to ask some questions about Aszal but I didn't want her to get the wrong idea. I didn't have to, she volunteered the information.

'Aszal's really nice, isn't he?'

'Yeah, he's all right, I suppose.' I could see that she was fishing. I wondered whether her mother had put her up to this.

'He really is a nice boy. Most of the girls in the youth group at church like him.'

'I'm sure they do.'

'Do you like him, Jas?' Cana thinks she's so smart.

'He's all right,' I said non-commitally. 'We don't have anything in common.'

46

'C'mon, tell the truth. I saw you both deep in conversation.'

'Actually he wanted to know about my nightmare.' I didn't bother to fill her in about him praying for me.

'Oh, he's so considerate.'

This got me wondering — did Cana fancy him? I asked her.

'I used to,' she said a bit too dreamily for my liking.

'What's that supposed to mean, you used to?'

'I've grown up, that's what it means. We were quite close at one time, and still are, and I thought, well, perhaps him and me . . . But I could see that God was leading us both in different directions, so what's the point in kicking against the goads?'

'The what?'

'Oh, it's something in the Bible. It just means what's the point of going against the grain? Just relax and flow with the waves.'

'Hmm, I like that, just flow with the waves. Sounds good.'

Cana gasped. 'Would you use that line in one of your raps?'

I grinned. 'Maybe.'

Cana continued about Aszal. 'He lives with his mother and younger brother Tukah.'

'Where do they come from?'

Cana laughed. 'See? You are interested.'

'Yeah, well, I suppose I am a bit, but not how you think. I mean having a name like Aszal Christa whatever it is, speaks for itself. Anyone with an enquiring brain would be interested.'

She nodded. 'Okay, even though you aren't really interested I'll tell you.' She grinned.

I sat still, trying to give the impression that I wasn't all that bothered.

'Aszal's eighteen. He wants to be a doctor . . . '

'Where's his dad?'

'He died four years ago.'

'That's a shame. How?'

'For the benefit of someone who isn't interested, he was killed in Cyprus. I'm not sure how, I just know it nearly killed his mother − shock and all that − and Aszal never spoke for ages and you hardly saw the family for months and then one day they all turned up in church as though nothing had happened. He is a very deep person.'

'Funny you should say that, but I sensed this, eh, this − I can't really explain it but it felt as though he had this feeling of mystery about him.'

Cana looked at me, not saying anything at first and then continuing the conversation as though I hadn't spoken. 'His father was from Cyprus hence Christodoulou, and his mother is English on her father's side and French Arabian on her mother's.'

'Wow. What a mixture!' Cana flashed me a look that stopped any more words falling out of my mouth.

'Where was I? Oh yes. He hasn't got a girlfriend, unless he's hiding her.' She looked at me slyly.

Just like her mother, I thought, but I didn't speak.

I began to feel sleepy as Cana droned on and on. I don't even remember snuggling under the duvet. I do remember feeling a bit apprehensive in case the nightmare returned, but it obviously wasn't a big worry as the next thing I knew birds were tweeting outside the window.

If it hadn't been for the sign in bold black lettering across the front of the church, The Mission Pentecostal Church, I would have thought it was a community hall or something.

It felt a bit like going to school when we trooped in through the double glass doors. Just inside, quite a few people were milling around. Some nodded their heads at Judy and Aubrey. I fixed my eyes on the notice board, not to read the notices but because I didn't want to talk to anyone. It didn't work. An old lady with lank grey hair and runny blue eyes came over.

'Hello, my dears.' She smiled, and I could see that her false teeth didn't fit properly.

'Hello, Mary. How are you?' asked Judy.

'Not so good, but God makes a way.' She turned to me, still smiling. I grinned for a second.

Judy introduced us.

'Oh, this is the little black orphan girl you have so kindly taken in.'

I went mad. People started looking at me. 'What do you mean little black orphan girl? What do you know about me anyway you nosy old — ?'

'That's enough, Jas,' said Judy.

'Oh, that's enough, is it?' I turned on Judy. 'I suppose I can thank you for blabbing my business all over the place.'

People were gasping and muttering in the background. I didn't care.

'Now listen, Jas. That's not true, I — '

Not giving her a chance to explain, I dived into her feet first (something I had been itching to do), knowing it could cause a lot of damage. 'So it's not true. Then how does she — ' I pointed to the old woman — 'know about me? Carrier pigeon or ESP? You lot call yourselves Christians — in whose eyes? I don't believe it's God, it's by your own standards. You're a bunch of two-faced hypocrites, just wanting to know other people's business and — '

Aubrey stepped forward. 'Come on, Jas.' He guided me gently by my arm. 'We will finish this conversation outside.'

My heart was beating a rhythm that, if played in a disco, would've set the place on fire. I was so hot I was glad to be going outside.

It was somewhat disconcerting walking slowly up the road with Aubrey on one side and Judy on the other. If a firing squad had jumped out on us and shot me I would not have been surprised.

Instead Aubrey stopped and said: 'What was all that about, Jas?'

Words failed me just when I needed them most.

49

Judy was looking across the road or more than likely waiting to hear my reply. I bet she was happy now that I had verbally attacked her.

'Well?' asked Aubrey.

Well may you ask, said my mind but not my mouth.

'Look Jas,' said Judy quietly, 'I know it's early days yet and you're among strangers and your mum's – '

'You leave my mum out of this,' I snarled. Why was I so upset? I couldn't understand it.

Aubrey sighed. 'If it is too much for you living with us – do you want to change? We could speak to Brenda.'

'No I don't.' I must be off my head. Why did I say no when for the last thirty-six hours all I've been thinking about is getting as far as possible away from this gang of religious nutters?

'No?' repeated Judy in surprise.

Ha ha. She wanted to get rid of me, I could tell. 'Yeah, that's right. I don't want to go.'

'If that's the case, then tell me why the big explosion.' Aubrey turned to face me. Something in his eyes made me realise that here was a dangerous man.

'I, hmm, I wasn't feeling myself.'

They both stared at me.

'And, hmm, I wasn't too happy to hear some old lady calling me a quote little black orphan unquote. Both my parents are still alive, you know,' I said, raising my voice.

Actually that *was* the bit that made me blow my top – orphan, cheek!

'I'm sorry about that, Jas.' An apologetic tone didn't suit Judy's voice. 'I only mentioned it to the prayer group that I attend. So does Mrs Rogers who's a little deaf and she obviously misunderstood.'

'Prayer group, you say. Well, as far as I'm concerned it sounds like a gossip group where everybody's business is discussed.' I wanted Aubrey to see what kind of a person he had married – an interfering supposedly 'do-gooder'. Fostering children to mess up their lives. It was all there churning away in my stomach ready to come out. It felt like a volcano on the verge of erupting.

'Okay. Let's call it a day and agree we're all sorry for it happening. Friends.' Aubrey smiled at me.

I smiled back.

'Friends, Jas.' Judy smiled too.

I gave her a half-second grin.

'Let's go,' said Aubrey, linking his arms through both of ours.

The service had already started. Everyone was on their feet singing at the top of their voices. I couldn't see Cana and Matt anywhere. The place was packed. Must have been a hundred people there, easily, and, something I wasn't expecting, there were people of every colour.

The church was quite deceptive. Looking from the outside, you wouldn't think the inside was so big. The seats were set out in rows forming a semi-circle. At the front was a table, a few chairs and a large wooden cross suspended from the ceiling. It was very bare.

Judy led the way and then all of a sudden she stopped, and began to make her way into a row of seats. Cana was already there, no Matt.

Cana handed me a hymn book with a smile. I felt embarrassed. It made me hot all over to stand there with Cana on one side and Judy on the other, holding a hymn book. I didn't want to be in church, especially with this family. Running out seemed much more feasible than being stuck here!

The vicar or whoever was in charge told us to sit down. Thank goodness.

I have never been so bored and worn out in all my life. This man went on and on about some fishermen throwing their nets over the side of a boat and not catching any fish. Then Jesus comes along and tells them to throw it over the other side and they catch loads. People were shouting out Hallelujahs and Amens every second. Then this man who must've eaten the Bible many times over flicked from one

51

page to the other and the whole church managed to keep up with him.

Whenever a song was sung we had to stand up and then sit down again, like a Yo-Yo. What got me was when they prayed. They all prayed together, at the same time but doing their own thing. And I reckon they had all come out of a local mental hospital, because people were praying and waving their hands in the air and muttering away to themselves.

But what really spooked me out was when Cana, Judy and Aubrey started doing it too! It was too much. There was absolutely no way that I was going to do it, even when I discovered as I looked around that I was the odd man out! Too bad.

The low mumbling noise would've driven a weaker person to commit a crime. Very tempting, I thought, looking at Judy.

When the vicar (I later found out he was called the pastor – all the same to me!) said that the next song would be the last one, I could've jumped up and started waving my arms about with joy.

What happened next made me want to burst out laughing. It was a lively number, a bit folksy. People old and young began to dance. If someone had told me about all this jigging about in a church, I wouldn't have believed them, but seeing it for myself left me with no doubt that, as my mum says, 'There's more of them out than in.' People were kicking their heels, like at a barn dance, clapping and moving in an uncoordinated way. It made my day.

I was glad that the Fentons only clapped. The shame of them doing anything more would've been too much.

It took about an hour actually to get out of the church. I now know what the Queen feels like, having to shake people's hands and make polite conversation. I had worn all my jewellery (the junk sort), baggy trousers, short sweat-shirt to the waist and suede waistcoat over it.

Being with this church lot for a few days I should have

52

realised that coming to their church I would be meeting people of the same calibre. The most popular question was: 'Are you a Christian?' Followed by: 'Are you a relative?' And from those in the know: 'How long are you staying with the Fentons?'

No way could anyone convince me that these were not a bunch of nosy parkers!

I managed to slip outside and breathed in deeply. The day was bright and quite warm. Children were chasing each other and messing about. I wondered what Donelle and Rosa were doing. My spirits began to take a downward plunge. Even the thought of going to see Mum at the hospital couldn't lift them. I would've preferred to go alone, but that was now out of the question. I was debating with myself whether to take off and get a bit of time with her on my own when someone called my name.

It was Aszal. I had been trying to locate him in the church but with all those people it was impossible. I was glad he had found me.

'Hi,' I chirped brightly.

'Did you enjoy yourself?' He nodded towards the church.

I raised my eyebrows.

He laughed. 'Oh come on, it's not that bad. You'll get used to it.'

'I don't think so.'

Trying to think of something nice to say to him was using up all my brain energy. Anyway, he asked me what I did in my spare time. I was going to ask him why he wanted to know, but instead I began to tell him about the rap band. He seemed really interested.

'Aszal.'

We both turned round. Standing there looking like a well-matured film star, with long, black, straight hair and saucer-large brown eyes was, I presumed, his mum. I was right.

'Mum, this is Jas.'

She nodded her head towards me. I suppose that meant 'Hello Jas and how are you?'

53

'We have to go,' she said to Aszal.

He nodded. Turning to me, he said, 'Bye, Jas. Hope to see you soon.'

My mouth dropped open. I wanted to ask what he meant by that, if he did mean anything. Hmm. I was getting a bit too caught up with analysing what and how and why he said or did something. It'd have to stop.

Matt rushed up to me. 'There you are, we've been looking for you.'

'Thought I'd escaped?'

He became serious. 'Is that how you feel about us?'

I was taken aback. 'No, no, just joking.'

The others turned up and we walked to the car. Driving to the hospital was a silent affair. It seemed to me that they had been warned not to say anything to me in case they upset me. Well, it's better than their chatter, I thought.

But Aubrey did ask me how the church was.

'Fine.' I couldn't say any more than that.

As we walked down the ward looking for Mum's bed I had been trying to suss out a way of talking to her on her own. The only thing I could think of was just to come out and say I wanted to speak to her alone, but I knew that Mum would think that very rude of me.

When we got to her bed, my mind went blank and tears began to well up inside me. She looked so small propped up with all those pillows and she had a bag full of blood hanging up on a metal pole beside her with a long lead which carried the blood through into her arm. It scared me.

'Mum.' I felt like crying.

She tried to sit up.

'Here, let me give you a hand,' said Judy.

I wanted to throw my arms around her and bury my head in her neck. I couldn't, one because they were here and two because it would upset Mum. I just stood looking down at her like a dummy.

Judy spoke to Mum most of the time. I just stared. Cana tried to talk to me but I couldn't even attempt to answer, in case I began to cry.

It seemed like the visit was all over in two minutes. Judy kissed Mum on the cheek, followed by Cana. Matt and Aubrey just said goodbye. I hugged Mum tightly.

'They won't be doing the operation for a few days yet, darling. My blood's a bit weak and I have to be fit to have the operation.'

That sounded stupid. The whole point of Mum being in hospital was because she was unfit. I just wanted her to come home so that we could all be together again.

On the way home Cana and Matt tried to cheer me up. I wasn't interested, so they gave up.

The dinner Judy cooked was nice. Rice and peas and beef with butter beans and lots of pepper. I hadn't realised she could cook West Indian food. Even so I couldn't eat it; I wasn't hungry. Judy was a bit upset, probably because she had made an effort for me. I still couldn't eat it.

The window-ledge in the bedroom was the ideal place for me. I could think without interruptions. Cana came into the room a few times but she left me undisturbed. Good, I thought, she's finally got the message.

Just looking out of the window made me feel good. It's funny how simple things like that can clear your head.

Seeing Mum in the hospital had brought it home to me that her operation was quite serious. How was I going to get through the months ahead? If this family were supportive it would really help me. I must visit Donelle and Rosa. I wished for the hundredth time that we were together. If the three of us were staying here I could tolerate the family. In fact it would be easier than staying with Aunt Merri. That shows how bad it would've been at Aunt Merri's! What a choice I had.

Well, I decided, I'll have a talk with Brenda tomorrow and see what she comes up with.

Aszal's name came to mind. I suddenly thought it would be good to talk it over with him. Yeah, that's a good idea. First things first: how do I contact him without it being taken wrongly? Hmm, I must find a way.

7

'Jas, I really think you should hurry up or you'll be late for school,' Cana said worriedly.

Still taking my time getting dressed I told her to calm down, it was only school after all!

Later, when I was stuck in a traffic jam with only twenty-five minutes to go before school started, I wished that I had taken Cana's advice. The bus just wasn't moving! Anxiety was building up inside me. Once I got to Romford I had to get another bus to Walthamstow, which would take about half an hour.

This is dreadful, I fretted. I didn't think that there would be so much traffic on the roads at this time.

To school from my house usually took twenty minutes and if I was feeling really energetic about fifteen minutes on top of that for walking.

I strolled through the school corridors in deadly silence. Everyone was in class, except me. I was three-quarters of an hour late!

There was no point running and getting all hot and sweaty. Five or ten minutes wouldn't make the slightest bit of difference to my head of year, Mrs Drivenmore, who was quite cool and understanding (or so she would like to think) in all aspects of school life except – lateness. That was something I hadn't had much trouble with, until today.

She's going to run her mouth and *drive* me *more* (just like her name) up the wall, I knew.

I knocked on her door, wishing I was someplace else.
Her voice boomed out: 'Come in.' So I did.
She looked up at me. 'Yes?'
'I'm late.'
At first she didn't answer. Then she said: 'It's nearly ten o'clock.'
'Tell me something I don't know,' I wanted to say. If eyes were like mouths mine would have revealed all!
'I cannot believe, Jasmine, that you have the audacity to come to school at this hour and behave as though nothing was wrong,' she said without taking a breath. This was only the beginning.
'But Mrs Drivenmore, I had to come from Upminster and I didn't realise that it would take me so long.'
'Why are you coming from Upminster? You don't live there.'
As far as I knew, only the headmistress knew that Mum was in hospital and I was being fostered. She might have told some of the other teachers, but I wasn't sure. I didn't want to tell Mrs Drivenmore. I wondered if she knew and was playing it smart and hoping I would say something. Too bad — I wasn't going to tell her.
'I stayed there last night, that's why.'
She looked at me.
I looked at her.
'Is this going to be a regular thing?'
She knew.
'What do you mean, regular?'
'I mean, Jasmine, are you going to be late every day?'
'No.'
'Well, I hope not. Otherwise you'll be on report. You may go.' She went back to her paperwork.
Outside the door I breathed a sigh of relief. I had been let off lightly. Normally she shouted at the top of her voice and gave out some terrible punishment, like stay behind after school and do something stupid: for instance, tidy up the games cupboard (which could fit the whole of

58

Walthamstow inside it) — ultra wicked — or sort out the library books.

The punishment didn't seem to work as it was always the same girls doing it!

The two lessons before lunch breezed past. It was a double period of maths. Usually whatever the teacher said went through one earhole and out the other, but the way I was feeling today it didn't even get as far as one earhole.

At lunchtime I dashed down to the front hall to the pay-phone. I had to get in contact with Brenda before she went to lunch.

I bumped into Lisa on the stairs.

'Hi, Jas. How's it going?'

'Lisa, I can't stop . . . '

'What's the rush? You having lunch with us?'

'No, I can't. I've got to see someone. Wait for me after school by the gate. I've got to go.'

'Yeah, later,' Lisa shouted as I reached the bottom of the stairs.

There was someone already on the phone: a girl with brown frizzy hair which was all over the place. She pumped in a coin.

Right. That would be about three minutes.

She pumped in another one. Another three minutes. By this time I had started to pace up and down like a man waiting for his wife to give birth.

She was still chatting.

I tapped her on the shoulder and mouthed: 'You going to be long?'

'Wait a second,' she said into the mouthpiece, then, turning to me, 'This is a public phone, okay?' and resumed her conversation.

It's at times like this that I can understand why people kill!

My fists were balled and my eyes piercing the back of her head, marking out a point where my fist would make itself known, when she put the receiver down. I sighed.

'Some people have no consideration,' she huffed.

'Some people are selfish,' I hissed back.

It didn't make me feel any better to have to wait for Brenda to come to the phone. I had already pumped in twenty pence.

'Hello, Brenda. I wonder whether I could see you now?' I had my fingers crossed. 'Yes, I'm fine, but I can't tell you over the phone. Please, I need to see you now, during my lunch-break . . . Five minutes will do.' I knew that was a lie, it would take me longer than that to explain, but anything to get to see her. ' . . . Oh, that's great, Brenda, I'll be outside the school gates, bye . . . '

Walking slowly towards the gates I tried to sort things out in my mind. What was I going to say to Brenda?

I counted the points out on my fingers:

1. Being with a mixed family;
2. Judy in particular;
3. The church business;
4. Is there somewhere else I could go?

By the time she turned up I only had half an hour left for lunch. I would have to talk quickly.

'Hello, Jasmine. Jump in.'

'Hi, Brenda.'

The car pulled away from the kerb; it seemed to know where it was going. We stopped by the park.

'Right. What's the problem?'

My mouth felt dry. Even though I had worked it all out before, I still didn't know where to begin.

'Is it Judy?' Brenda asked.

I nodded.

'Listen, most of the kids I've placed with the Fentons all say the same things: Judy's bossy, she thinks she knows everything. But the trouble is that you can't or shouldn't judge a person from only knowing them a short while. She obviously does things differently from your mum, but honestly, underneath she has a heart of gold, and after a couple of weeks most of the kids settle down with hardly any problems.'

60

She looked at me.

I felt choked up, but I still wanted to explain how I felt. 'She's a nice woman, really she is.'

I swallowed. 'The thing is, Brenda,' I said, thinking back to my list of points, 'firstly, Judy's white and her husband's black. Why didn't you tell me? I was shocked.'

'Is that a problem for you, Jasmine?'

'No,' I almost shouted. 'It's not a problem for me, but I'm finding it hard to handle. Look, I haven't got anything as such against white people, but, they are different.'

Brenda laughed. 'Then what about me?'

'You're different.' I looked at her and then realised my mistake. 'I don't mean like that, but you're someone on my side, so to speak.'

'Oh, I see. It's a war then, if I have to take sides?'

I could see that this was going to be difficult. 'No, no, I don't mean it like that.'

'People are people no matter what colour they are,' said Brenda.

'Really. Would you be saying that to me if we lived in South Africa, or you were a member of the National Front?'

She couldn't answer me.

'Apart from that, there's this religious business. They are fanatics. All of them are brainwashed. I went to their church on Sunday and do you know what? — "kind-hearted" Judy had told my business to the whole congregation. I felt sick when I found out.'

'Did she?' Brenda frowned.

'Yes she did,' I spat out.

Taking a deep breath, she said: 'Jasmine, I know what you're going to say next. You want to move, right?'

'Yes.' At last I had got through.

'Okay, but the only thing I can offer you at this moment is the home.'

Feelings of hope that had started to lift up inside me sank down again. 'Please, Brenda. There must be somewhere else.'

'I'm sorry, Jasmine. You'll have to wait a couple of weeks at least before something will turn up. I'm really sorry that you haven't got on with the Fentons. They are nice people.'

I felt like crying.

'Have you seen your mum?'

Sniffing, I told her I had.

She put her arm around me, which just brought the tears to the surface. They flowed down my cheeks, racing to get to my jaw.

'Life is hard at the moment for you Jasmine, but it will get better. Please try and give the Fentons a little more time. Look, let's leave it a week. If by that time you really can't stand it any longer, we'll have to move you, right?'

'A week?' I whispered.

'Yes, a week. In the meantime, I'll try and find somewhere else for you. That's the most I can say now, all right?' Looking at her watch, she tutted. 'Time to go, I'm afraid. Dry your eyes.' She offered me a tissue from a packet.

I blew my nose noisily.

She handed me the packet. 'You might need these.'

As I was opening the car door and climbing out, Brenda said I could call her anytime.

During the last lesson, which was a free period because the teacher was off sick, I sat with my head in my hands. My mind was filled with incongruous thoughts all jumbled up together. I was deaf, dumb and blind to my surroundings. The rest of the class were chatting and fooling around, but no one came near me. A few girls had tried to speak to me, but when I was rude to them, they backed off. I didn't need pity or a shoulder to cry on. In fact I didn't know what I needed.

I just wanted my mum. How could I tell anyone that I — Jas, the girl who was *so* together, who wrote hard rap and knew all the answers — that I missed my mum and sisters?

When my dad first went away I had felt bad, really cut

up, but somehow — apart from a few bad nights — I had coped. This was different.

My biggest fear, which I couldn't even think about for too long, was my mum's operation. A dreadful thought that kept coming back to me, hitting me and forcing its way constantly into my mind, was: What if mum died? I knew that I would die too. I could not conceive of life without my mum. It might seem selfish, but I didn't care. If she died who would I talk to, who could I lean on? No one. I wouldn't be able to take it.

I thought guiltily of Donelle and Rosa. I hadn't even been considering how they would take it, how it would affect them. I was just concerned about myself.

The shrill ringing of the bell reverberated in my skull.

I felt sluggish, and as I stood up the ground seemed to jump at me.

'You all right, Jas?'

I pushed whoever it was away with my arm.

'Get the teacher,' someone said.

Arms forced me back down into the chair. I tried to struggle against them but they were stronger than me.

'Jasmine, can you hear me?'

I nodded and moved my lips: 'Yes.'

'What's wrong?'

Shaking my head, I took a lungful of air. My head seemed to clear, and my eyes focused on the faces around me.

'Have you eaten today?' asked Miss Blake.

I thought for a moment, then realised that I hadn't even had breakfast. 'No, I, eh, didn't have time.'

'Honestly, you young girls trying to lose weight are very stupid. Come on, you'll have to have a cup of tea or something.' She took my arm and helped me up.

After sitting me down in the staffroom with a cup of sweet tea, Miss Blake informed the other teachers that I had been starving myself, and the state that I was in now was the result. I didn't bother to explain. Let them think what they wanted to.

There was a knock on the door. It was Lisa. She rushed over to me.

'What's the matter, Jas?'

'She's been starving herself, stupid girl.'

Lisa screwed up her face. 'Jas starve herself?' She looked at Miss Blake then at me. 'I'll take Jas home, miss. She'll be all right with me.'

'No, that's okay, Lisa. I'll take her by car.'

I piped up quickly: 'No, no, it's okay, Miss Blake. Thanks all the same. I'll go to Lisa's house. Her mum will drop me off.'

Getting up a little unsteadily, I made for the door.

'I don't think that's wise, Jasmine.'

'I'm all right, honestly.' I smiled hoping to convince her that I was. She backed off.

All the way to Lisa's house I couldn't speak. She never probed or questioned me, which helped a lot — it gave me a chance to think straight.

Lisa's mum, who is just like my mum, phoned Judy straight away and told her that I had been taken sick at school and that it wasn't very serious and she would bring me home shortly. I was grateful that she spoke to Judy. The way I was feeling I couldn't have said two words to her that would've made any sense.

Upstairs in Lisa's bedroom we sat on the floor with the stereo on low. I felt relaxed for the first time in the last few days. The music was slow with a heavy beat — it was Bobby Brown at his best. His voice wrapped itself around me and seemed to draw out the bad feelings that were inside.

Breathing evenly I began to sense a nice glow light up inside me, but at the same time the situation I was in was threatening to take me over completely again. I tried to hold on to this nice feeling while I could.

'How you doing, Jas?' Lisa was really concerned. That in itself — that someone did care about me — made me feel better.

'So so.'

'Having a rough time of it, eh?' She stretched out her hand and squeezed my shoulder.

Tears again. I was beginning to get mad with myself. Why couldn't I control myself? I bent my knees and rested my head on them.

'It's your mum, isn't it? I know, it must be hard.'

Lifting my head, I looked at Lisa, and moved my lips trying to form words.

'Don't try and speak.'

'No, no' I said breathlessly. 'I want to talk, I need to talk, I feel like I'm going to burst like a balloon and splatter all over the place if I don't.'

Lisa leant back against the bed and let me carry on.

'I'm frightened, Lisa. What if my mum died?' There. I had said it, not that it left me feeling any better.

'She's not going to die, Jas. Try and not think about it. I know it must be hard but you'll drive yourself mad.'

'Oh, Lisa, it's driving me mad now. There's just nothing I can do about it. I feel so helpless.'

Neither of us spoke for a while. The music rocked on filling the empty spaces. When it came to an end Lisa made a move towards the stereo to turn the LP over. I stopped her. 'I need to talk to you.'

She held up her hand. 'No, let me say something first. I know this hasn't got anything to do with it, but in five weeks time the Metro are holding a rap competition. We stand a good chance of winning, but we have to be ace.' She made the letter 'O' with her thumb and forefinger.

'Really? That'll be great.' The information brought a little smile to my face.

I started telling Lisa about the Fentons: Aubrey first, then Matt and Cana and finally Judy.

'You really are having a hard time, Jas.' She shook her head.

'Imagine having all that aggro on top of the worry of my mum being in hospital, the girls at Aunt Merri's who doesn't understand or even like kids and my dad being thousands of miles away.'

'I wish you could stay here.'

'Yeah, so do I. But that's out of the question.'

'This black and white business, it is hard to understand. I just couldn't see myself with a white guy, could you?'

'No way. I couldn't even bring myself to chat normally, let alone anything else.' Aszal's face popped into my mind. My mouth closed instantly.

Lisa looked at me. 'You all right?'

'Yeah. Fine.'

Lisa flipped the LP over.

Aszal's name fixed itself in my head. I couldn't get rid of it. Reasoning with myself, I thought: Strictly speaking, Aszal is white, and if Lisa met him she would definitely say something about him not being black! Anyway, he isn't my boyfriend or anything — there's no chance of that as far as I'm concerned. He's just a friend.

We had a good laugh when I told her about going to church. Lisa was screaming with laughter when I mimicked the way the people were dancing. It was funny.

'Oh Jas, I'll have to come one day. It sounds out of this world.'

It was.

Lisa's mum came into the room. 'Sorry to spoil your fun, girls. I've got to go and straighten someone's hair, so I'll have to take you home now, Jas, all right?'

'Yeah, okay, Mrs Victor.'

Turning the car off at Romford and heading towards Upminster, Mrs Victor asked me about the Fentons.

'Oh boy, Mum. What a loaded question! Jas can't tell you everything now.'

'What? Are they ill-treating you?'

'No they're not, but it's a different kind of family,' I said. I told her about Judy being white and Aubrey black.

66

'That's wrong, the social services should have put you with a black family, made you feel at home. Does your mum know?'

'Yeah, she does, but we haven't had a chance to speak because when I visited her they came with me.'

'Probably to check on you so you don't say the wrong thing.'

As the car turned into the Fentons' road, I asked Lisa and her mum cautiously what colour they thought Greek people or Arabs were. Mrs Victor thought that Arabs were black people, and she wasn't sure about Greeks.

'Yeah, I consider Arabs to be black people. I think that's how they feel themselves,' Lisa said. 'That's the part of the world that Jesus was supposed to come from, but the way he's portrayed you would think he was English.'

'Just in front of this blue car,' I instructed Lisa's mum. She stopped.

'Why did you want to know, Jas?'

'Hmm, nothing. I was just interested.'

'Well, as for Greeks, as far as I'm concerned,' Lisa went on, 'in this country they're ethnic minorities.'

We all laughed. Ethnic minorities was not our favourite way to be described.

'It's a big house they've got, Jas,' said Mrs Victor.

'Yeah. It's quite nice actually.'

'Pity about the family, though,' sighed Lisa.

'Hmm.'

As I got out of the car Lisa asked me if we would be meeting as usual on Wednesday, so she could tell BB. I said yes.

The porch light flashed on and the front door opened. Judy came out. 'Hi, Jas. You all right?'

The way she said it I knew that she knew. Either the school or Brenda had been on to her, or both. I didn't care at that moment.

'This is my friend, Lisa, and her mum, Mrs Victor.'

They all said hello and talked politely for a few minutes.

Then Mrs Victor turned the car around and drove up the road.

Judy smiled at me, and stretching out her arm, guided me towards the house. She made me feel uncomfortable. All the things I had been saying and thinking about her somehow seemed small and insignificant.

'Do you want to straighten up before tea?'

'Eh, yeah. Okay.' I climbed the stairs slowly.

As I opened the bedroom door a strong feeling of homesickness hit me. Cana was sitting up in bed doing her homework. She could afford to feel comfortable, this was her home. It wasn't mine.

I plonked down on the bed, my school bag still on my shoulder and my jacket on.

Cana looked up at me. She smiled and went back to her books.

She didn't seem herself. She knows too, I realised.

Suddenly I felt like a criminal. I couldn't help feeling the way that I did about mixed relationships. It wasn't my fault that my mum was ill. It wasn't my fault about a lot of things that I couldn't change — but did I have to accept them?

'Aunt Myrtle's coming here at the end of the week, Jas,' Cana piped up.

'Is she?' I stood up, dropped my school bag to the floor and took off my jacket.

'You'll get on well with her. Give her a little while and you'll find out she's really a scream.'

'Hmm.'

I knew she was saying that to pacify me.

A week, Brenda said. A lot can happen in a week. I'll just have to see.

8

We've got something to tell ya
That we think you should know,
It's a message for the young
And the middles and the old.
So don't back off and think it's
Not for you,
It's bigger than life
And it
Can kill you.
So stop
Look
And listen to this –
We're gonna open our mouths
And use our lips.

Now don't *now don't*
Let the power *let the power*
Take you over *take you over*
And con-trol ya *con-trol ya*

NOWDON'TLETTHEPOWERTAKEYOUOVER

'It sounds wicked, Jas,' said BB grinning from ear to ear.

'The lyrics are crucial, really ace.' Lisa punched the air
with her right hand.

I was pleased that they were pleased. It boosted my
confidence to know that even though the last few days had

been hard for me, I had managed to write the rap.

Ever since Monday things had seemed a bit different in the house. Everyone was polite to me, not that they weren't before but I got the feeling that words had been spoken to the family as a whole and they were laying off me. I did feel somewhat guilty as I thought that they were walking around me as if I was a World War Two bomb that might go off any minute. After all it was their house!

Cana told me that Aszal and his mum and brother were coming for tea on Friday, at which my heart jumped, but I was as cool as a cucumber outwardly. Aunt Myrtle was coming home on Friday too. Full house!

'This is the rap that's going to win the competition, you know?' BB was nodding her head.

'We need to practise like mad and really get it hot. It's going to mash the place up, drive people wild. I know, I can feel it.' Lisa blew a bubble from the gum she had been chewing since we finished school two hours ago.

'You have to get the scratching tighter, BB — it's dragging a bit,' I told her.

'Don't worry Jas, leave it with me. I know what I'm doing.'

BB is a pretty girl. No, not pretty — *beautiful*! She's about five foot eight without shoes. With shoes she's ten foot! Well, it seems like it. Her skin colour can only be described by one word: 'Midnight'. Sometimes when the light catches her it seems to glow a blue-black. She's slim and walks like a panther. Some people in our school were a bit scared of her, just because of her looks. She holds herself up tall, never stooping or sloppy, just like a model. Funny thing though, she has small hands and feet. Her hair was platted and twisted into long ringlets down to the small of her spine, and she tied brightly-coloured cloths round her head.

The teachers at school couldn't handle her. I admit she was what might be termed rebellious, but we are all individuals. And as far as I'm concerned, school is a place

70

that just wants to crush the living daylights out of you! That won't be happening to BB.

'I've got to shoot off now girls. I'm going to see my mum in hospital.'

'How is she?' asked BB.

'She'll be having her operation on Friday,' I said quietly. I had been trying not to think about it. I could see that Friday was going to be a very stressful day for me.

'Look, don't bother to help us clear things away, Jas. You go and see your mum now and leave everything to us.'

'You sure, Lisa?' I looked at BB. 'Are you sure too?'

'Yeah, you go on. Leave it, right?' said BB.

'Thanks. You've both been really good to me. I really appreciate it.'

Mum was off the drip. I could see her sitting up as I walked down the ward. She smiled at me. She looked brighter too.

'You look great, Mum.' I kissed her cheeks. She smelled all nice and soapy.

'I feel good. This rest is doing me the world of good. How are you?'

'Fine.'

I sat in the chair near the bed and Mum and I looked at each other, not saying a word.

It's funny: I have never really looked closely at Mum. I suppose when you see someone every day you tend not to bother with things like 'getting to know them'. You feel you already do!

Mum's eyes were twinkling. Her face glowed brighter too, and for a woman her age she hardly had any lines. Her skin looked so soft, like a ripe peach — you just wanted to stretch out and squeeze it gently.

Mum smiled at me and I was surprised to see two faint dimples appear. Well, I had never seen them before. As she smiled her eyes looked sort of hazy — if I was a man I might have begun to think that she was making a pass at me!

'How's the Fentons?' she asked. 'They seemed such a nice family.'

I didn't know what to say. If I told Mum how I felt I knew that she would be worrying about me, which wouldn't be good for her condition. But I wanted to say something.

'They are all right, but − but I wish I had known about them before.'

'What do you mean?' Mum asked with a note of concern in her voice.

'Well.' Here we go, I thought. Tread carefully. 'The first thing is so obvious . . .'

'What?' Alarm bells ringing in Mum's tone.

'Eh, the black and white business.'

Mum sighed. 'Oh that's nothing. I thought they were ill-treating you or something.'

'But Mum, it gave me such a shock when I met Judy and then when I met her husband − well, I just couldn't believe it.'

Mum smiled at me. She stretched out her arm and stroked my hair. 'You are so funny sometimes. One minute you're like a big woman, and the next you're like a little girl.'

'Mum!'

'Well, it's true. I knew you would react that way when you found out.'

'What? You knew about it?'

Mum nodded.

That threw me. There was I expecting her to side with me about the situation, when she knew it all along. 'But Mum, I don't think it's right. And in any case, why did you let me go to them, knowing that I don't like mixed marriages? I didn't think you did either.'

'Jasmine. What people do with their lives is their business. When Brenda first told me about the Fentons I wasn't too happy because for one, hearing you and your friends go on about black and white relationships being wrong, I knew you would say no and I was worried that if you refused the Fentons you might have to go into the home. And secondly,

72

though *I* haven't anything against mixed marriages, I was just concerned about you living amongst people you didn't know, and what they would be like, how they would treat you, would they take the time to understand you — things like that. But my hands are tied. Seriously though, Jas, what would you have preferred, them or the home?'

Not waiting for me to answer, Mum carried on: 'Your dad agreed that even though the family were mixed they seemed decent people. I liked the fact that they were churchgoers.'

'Mum, how could you let me stay with a bunch of religious nutcases?'

She laughed out loud, revealing pearly white teeth. Laughing made her look years younger. Pity that she was laughing at something that I couldn't even smile about.

'Jasmine, if you could see yourself you would laugh too. As for them being a bunch of religious fanatics, they believe in God and Jesus and not some airy fairy religion that has people giving all their money away or doing strange things. Anyway, you know your father and I believe in Jesus, and you could be doing some praying for me while you're there — I need all the help I can get to see me through this operation.'

'Lisa's mum thinks it's wrong for me to be with the Fentons.'

At first Mum didn't answer me, then she said: 'Listen Jasmine, you'll be sixteen soon. No longer a child, a woman. Why, if I let you, you could be married . . .'

'Oh yeah, but would you let me marry a white boy?'

'I wouldn't let you marry anyone at sixteen. But listen. The older you are the more experience in life you have, and I have come to the conclusion that colour is something political. It helps to win votes and keeps people divided. Think of all the white people you know, are they really that bad?'

'Yeah, loads of them and — '

'As I was saying,' Mum looked at me, 'take my advice,

73

Jasmine, and try and live a good life and get on with all the people you meet. Life's too short. Look at me now, if it wasn't for the Fentons I would be more ill than I am, worried that you were in a home with all sorts of people, maybe even getting into trouble.'

I looked at her not wanting to believe what I had just heard. How could she be so calm and uncaring about my staying with the Fentons? I could see that it would be useless to push the point that I wasn't very happy with the situation. I'd just have to drop it for now.

'Aunt Myrtle, their aunt, is coming out of hospital on Friday and she'll be staying with us.'

'Aunt Myrtle? Who's she?'

'It's Aubrey — that's the dad — it's his great-aunt or something. She fell over and broke her foot.'

'Poor thing.'

'You're joking, Mum: poor thing? She's a right warrior. The first time we met she said to me "Are you a Christian an saved by Jesus?" I wanted to laugh.'

'Ha ha, you've got the accent good, Jasmine. She sounds like my mother.' Mum kept laughing.

I was glad that Mum was happy; knowing that she was going to have a major operation in two days' time, she was still able to joke and laugh.

'Have you seen Donelle and Rosa yet?'

'No Mum, but I have spoken to them over the phone. I don't think they're too happy with Aunt Merri. Mind you, I don't think I would be either.'

'Now look at that. You are probably better off at the Fentons than you would've been at Aunt Merri's.'

I couldn't say anything to that. In fact there was no comparison.

'What's the time, Jasmine?'

Looking at my watch, I told Mum it was five to seven.

'You had better go now.'

'Mum, it's not late. Look how bright it is outside.'

'I know, Jasmine, that it's early to you, but remember

that you're staying with people and you can't just come and go as you please. Besides, if I was at home you know I wouldn't stand for that.'

'You're still the same, Mum.' I smiled.

'You don't think being in hospital would've changed me?' I laughed.

'Now be a good girl. If they ask you to go to church you go and pray for me . . . '

'Talking about church, when I went on Sunday some old lady came up to me and asked me if I was the little black orphan girl that the Fentons were looking after. What a cheek!'

'Where did she get that from?'

'Judy reckons that she told them about me in her prayer group — more like a meeting to talk about people's business.'

'Hmm. I remember prayer meetings at church when I was a young girl in Jamaica. People were supposed to be praying for each other or someone they knew who had a need or they felt they were carrying a burden for, but instead it was more like disclosing other people's business. But I don't think Judy was gossiping.'

'Mum, you don't know her. There's something not quite right about Judy. She's the sort of person who wants everyone to think she's nice, but underneath she's sly.'

Mum looked thoughtful. 'She seemed so nice and concerned. People are so funny, one minute you think you know them and then they do something that shocks the life out of you, Jasmine, just be careful around that woman. Don't get into any argument. It's her house and family, you are a guest. Just let her carry on doing what she knows best how to do. Any problems, tell Brenda.'

'Brenda's her friend.'

'Oh Lord, nothing but problems.'

I could see that Mum was getting worried. Feeling guilty, I wondered how I could stop her worrying. 'Just before I go, Mum, my rapping group are entering a competition, and

I've written a new rap, it's brilliant and — '

'You and this rap business. I hope you're just as enthusiastic for your school work, young lady.'

'Mum, we are going to win.' I bunched my fists and shook them.

A nurse came along and asked Mum if she wanted a cup of tea.

'Yes, thanks dear.'

'Okay Mum, I'm off.'

We hugged each other like bears for what seemed hours. It felt nice to be hugged by Mum.

'Eh, Mum, what colour do you think Arabs are, or Greek people?'

'What is the matter now, Jasmine? What is your problem with colour?'

'It isn't my problem. It's mainly white people having a problem with people with black skin; they seem to need to classify people by shade or tone. I was just wondering what colour you, personally, would call people of those races.'

'I would call them beautiful. God created them so they must be good. Now off you go, and phone the hospital when you get there so that I know that you're safe.'

We kissed.

At the door of the ward I turned and waved. Mum waved back.

On the bus going back to Upminster I had a lot to think about. If we won the rap competition it would be a big step forward in being recognised. I thought we stood a good chance. It was the *in* thing now to be girl rappers and not only did I think we were good, on stage we looked good too.

For Mum's sake I would try and keep a low profile at the Fentons, only it isn't easy, I've discovered, living with people and doing your own thing. I would've loved to know why Aubrey married Judy; finding out might not be that difficult with Aunt Myrtle coming to stay. I hoped she'd lay off the 'become a Christian' campaign. If she did we could become friends, I thought.

Aszal. Even his name had a ring to it. I liked him a lot. I had been searching my brain to see if I had ever felt like that with anyone else, and the only person I could think of was Robert. But with him no sooner did I start feeling a stirring in my heart for him, than he put me off by telling people I fancied him! Just proving to me how immature he was.

Aszal seemed different. I didn't like his mum much. She seemed to think she was a cut above everyone else, but that was no problem. Something that was a problem was his appearance. What would my friends think if they saw me with a 'white boy'? Anyway he was Christian, and I wasn't sure how he felt about me. He seemed friendly enough. And besides, as Mum says: I'm too young to be thinking of marriage and stuff.

But still, who knows what can happen?

9

I was so glad that school was over. Thursdays were the
worst. Double maths and French before lunch and then
geography and sociology in the afternoon. Whoever had
planned the timetable obviously had no understanding of
young minds. Too much studying is bad for you I'm sure.
Most of the lessons had been a blur anyway. I had too much
on my mind.

Friday was going to be an action-packed day, what with
Mum's operation and Aunt Myrtle coming home and Aszal
and family coming round — even the rap competition was
buzzing around in my head. How my brain hadn't burst yet
was beyond my comprehension.

I was leaning against the bus stop concentrating on the
lyrics of the rap I had written — too busy to notice anything
or anyone around me.

'Hi Jas.'

'. . . So stop, look and listen to —'

'Hey,' shouted a voice. I snapped back to reality.

It was Robert.

'Hi.' I smiled.

'What's happening, Jas? Long time no see.'

I shrugged my shoulders.

'What does that mean?' he asked.

'Not much.'

'C'mon, I know you too well. There's always excitement
when you're around.'

The way he said that and the look he gave me made me

feel all funny inside. I wondered if he still liked me. I found it hard to look him in the eye, in fact I felt stupid.

I felt even worse as my bus roared past. I didn't even have a chance to stick my hand out to stop it. What a nuisance!

'Nothing's happening, just boring life,' I said to the back of the bus. Missing that bus would mean that I was going to be late home. What a drag!

'Well, you look good for it. Very nice indeed.' He stared at me directly, causing me to stare back at him.

He's a head taller than me, with short cropped hair. Brown eyes that are so dark they are almost black. Even though he was eighteen there was no sign of any facial hair, his skin looked so smooth — like a pebble. I knew that some women would pay loads of money to have skin like it.

'So, where are you off to?'

'Home.'

'Home? Wrong direction.'

I'd forgotten for a moment that I was going to the Fentons — they seemed miles away, another planet in fact.

'Oh, I'm staying with some friends of my mum's while she's in hospital.' (Lying seemed to come so easily — well, it was only a half-lie — it rolled easily off my tongue.)

He grinned. 'Could I have the number? I'd like to give you a ring some time, it would be nice to meet up — and who knows?'

Suspicion crept into my voice. I knew how conniving Robert could be.

'Who knows what?'

Very coolly, he said, 'Just to get acquainted.'

I wasn't too sure what he meant by acquainted. I didn't really want to know. After what happened the last time with him blabbing his mouth about me I had to protect myself in case it happened again.

We spent the time laughing and joking. I must admit he is good company: he knows how to crack a joke. I began comparing him with Aszal. It wasn't something that I purposely thought about — it just happened. They were like

79

chalk and cheese. Well, one is black and the other is, hmm, sort of white. One was a Christian and the other wasn't, which was cool for me, because the thought of spending the rest of my life in church with a bunch of hypocritical mad people wasn't very appealing. I'd rather be in a night club getting down to some serious moves!

Glancing at my watch, I groaned: twenty minutes had gone by already. Judy was going to be uptight to say the least. She wasn't able, it seemed, to handle anything that upset her routine. I wanted to laugh out loud − to think that now I was part of someone's routine.

I remembered last week when Cana had come home an hour late. Judy didn't even give her a chance to explain; she just calmly (or so it seemed) told her in plain English how annoyed she was and that Cana wouldn't be going out at the weekend to some gathering with her mates − which wasn't funny as I was supposed to be going with her, something that Judy obviously wasn't concerned about.

I was wondering how she was going to react to me coming home late, when I was interrupted by Robert's insistent voice. 'Who is he?' he joked.

'Who is he? What are you going on about?'

'He must be nice to be filling your brain so much that you can't communicate with anyone.'

'Robert, what's with the riddles, eh?'

'Well Jas, I've been talking to you and you just haven't been there.'

'For your information, I haven't got a boyfriend and I was wondering where the bus was.'

He seemed to like that answer.

'Eh Jas, what are you doing on Saturday?'

I wasn't able to answer him as the bus seemed to appear from nowhere.

'Have you got a pen and paper, quick?' I asked

He pulled them out of his pocket like a magician pulls a rabbit out of a hat. I told him the number and he wrote it down quickly.

I turned to him as I got on the bus and said, 'Call me soon.'

He nodded. 'You bet.'

As the bus drove off, I didn't turn back to wave or anything. I wanted to appear cool and laid back — otherwise he'd get too full of himself thinking that I was desperate for a boyfriend. And was I?

Not really, I thought. Having a good friend who just happened to be a boy would be nice though, as long as he didn't get fresh! It would make a nice change having a boy for a friend. Sometimes girls can be very spiteful to each other, and there always seems to be rivalry whenever boys are around.

The situation between Nina and Lisa came to me very clearly. Some guy called Leon, otherwise known as 'Rapper Lee', fancied Lisa. We all knew this, Nina included. Lisa was taking it easy and relaxed, doing things properly, when big-mouthed Nina went and told Leon that Lisa wasn't interested. The stupid fool believed her and backed off.

We couldn't understand why all of a sudden, whenever Leon was around, Nina would play up to him and he would ignore Lisa. Somehow Lisa found out and she was mad. We all were. No one spoke to Nina — we just blanked her.

That is what I mean about being among girls.

If you had a boy for a friend and you were able to confide in him that you liked someone, there would be no competition between you. If he knew the guy he might even put in a nice word.

But the question remained — did I want a boyfriend? I wondered what Aszal would be like as a boyfriend. Does he know how to treat girls? Is he considerate and sensitive? Is he the 'green-eyed' kind of guy? I wondered if parting with his money was a problem. All these questions seemed to spring out at me from nowhere. And the answer came quickly and simply: I'm not planning to marry the guy so it's no big deal what he's like. I don't want to get married anyway. It's a dead-end, thankless job and no woman in her right mind would want it.

Feeling satisfied with myself I settled back in my seat. The bus was going nowhere. Looking down the aisle through the front window, I could see the traffic was stationary. I'd be home in time for the *Nine O'Clock News* at this rate. Judy would have a blue fit. She would probably have called the police by then, thinking I couldn't stand any more of them and had run away, or perhaps someone had kidnapped me!

I smiled to myself — I certainly wouldn't give her the satisfaction of thinking that I couldn't cope, and had done a moonlight! No way. I'm staying put. Talk about can't make your mind up. One minute I wanted to leave and the next I wanted to stay. Well, they say that the adolescent years are the most difficult. I agree.

It began to rain. Slowly at first: small drops of water gently tap, tapping at the window, and then gradually faster, as though someone was turning up the water pressure, until big drops were falling fast and furiously.

It was amazing. One minute it was a nice spring evening, the next it was like being under a high-speed shower. The sky had got darker. This is weird, I thought. But then the English weather is known throughout the world for being unpredictable!

My watch said 4.35. Usually at this time the bus was at Newby Park. Instead we hadn't even reached Wanstead.

I was truly bored. I didn't even have a magazine or an interesting book that I could pass the time with. Closing my eyes, I leaned against the window-pane. The rain's patter vibrated around my head. It was an even beat. I began to tap my toes.

Trying to think up words that could go with the beat was a bit difficult at first. I wasn't one hundred per cent comfortable and relaxed. I needed to be to let the words flow.

Slowly words began bubbling up in my mind, literally

82

from nowhere. I wasn't even sure what they were, then they registered. My heart leapt. I couldn't believe that I had memorised them:

> For God so loved the world
> That
> He gave His
> One and only Son
> I said that
> God so loved the world
> That
> He gave His
> One and only Son.

Wow! This was incredible. Where had I picked up those words? My brain cells were crashing into one another — I could feel them rushing around trying to figure out the puzzle. Never, in all my history of writing rap music, had I ever thought about God. I didn't believe it.

'Those posters,' I said aloud.

The man in front of me turned and looked at me strangely.

My instant reaction was to open my mouth to tell him I wasn't mad. Instead I closed it. Protesting one's innocence wasn't always the wisest thing.

Back to the rap. I must have unconsciously remembered them. The words were as clear as a bell. Why had I recalled them so clearly? I thought hard about it, and my dream of being in the dark room vividly sprang into focus.

I didn't want to think about it. There had been times since I had dreamt it when I could sense the memory of it coming back to me, but I had busied myself doing something, anything so that I wouldn't think about it. But now, unfortunately, stuck on the top of this bus which was going nowhere, with nothing else to do, I couldn't get rid of it.

If only I could walk about, or sing at the top of my voice or talk to someone, I knew that the dream would be quickly erased from my mind. But I couldn't do anything.

For God so loved the world . . . the golden box . . . that He gave His one and only Son . . . the handleless door, the dark room.

Round and around in my mind it went. I could feel my arms and legs quivering with goosepimples. This was getting scary. What with the rain and the sky so full of clouds, it was dark and dismal. The bus was creeping along as though it was afraid to go faster. I wished I was someplace else.

Being on the bus seemed like the dream – locked in and going nowhere. Waves of panic gushed over me. I wanted to scream. My seat became uncomfortable. I started to wriggle about.

For God so loved the world for God so loved the world for God so loved the world.

I wondered for a moment if I was going round the bend. It was definitely living with the Fentons, they were a family of nutcases. I'm sure madness is contagious.

All this business about God. They made God seem such a big issue. So what? He loved the world, big deal. I love the world, I'm sure that most people love the world, that's why nobody wants to die.

I was trying to get a grip on myself. I thought that letting the words go over and over in my mind would make me realise just that – that they were words and nothing else.

The picture of the man holding the lamb in his hands came to me. Okay, so that's Jesus. I knew that he was supposed to be a kind and easy-going guy, that he loved animals and children. Yeah, so what? So do I and loads of other people.

He gave His one and only Son.

At first I couldn't work that bit out: gave His one and only Son. Then somehow I knew what it meant. Easter. Jesus dying on the cross, but why? Hmm.

He must have done something wrong, or he was wrongly found guilty and so he was killed. But that happens the world over, people being murdered just for being themselves.

84

I felt that was the answer.

So being a Christian is what? Believing in God and Jesus. Father and Son.

I was sure that a lot of people believed in God. My mum did, and was she a Christian? Yes, as far as I could see. But she didn't carry on like the Fentons.

Bunch of nutters. In fact the whole church was full of crackpots. Jumping about like they had taken some artificial stimulant!

The dark room in my dream flashed back into my head. Now I'm not a dreamy sort of person. Usually I go to bed and sleep. No dreams, no nightmares, no interrupted sleep. Just pure sleep.

Until that afternoon. Well, that's something I wouldn't be doing again in a hurry, sleeping in the middle of the day. But I must admit, I did feel that the dream meant something.

Mum's a great one for dreams. She tells me them the next morning, and sometimes the meaning, which she looks up in her dream book.

So the dream I had must have a definite meaning. What? Being locked in somewhere and not being able to get out. The Fentons. A ghost of a smile licked my lips. Yet this whole situation had a very serious feel to it. Or was I making something out of nothing?

I looked out of the window. The sky had cleared and the rain had stopped as quickly as it had started. The bus was at Gants Hill. The time was 5.05.

A young black woman came and sat next to me. She smiled. I smiled back. I liked that. It's nice when a perfect stranger smiles at you, unthreatening, just being friendly. She got a book out.

I nestled down as best I could in my seat and thought about Rosa and Donelle. I must phone them tonight. I wondered if they missed me. I sure did miss them. It's funny, how much people take each other for granted. The girls both got on my nerves when we were at home, yet being away from them left a gap in my life. I wondered how Aunt Merri was handling them. She's a real sergeant major.

I glanced at the girl next to me who was heavily into her book, though I had noticed that she hadn't turned any pages. I sort of turned slightly in my seat to see what she was reading. My eyes nearly fell out of my head. At the top of the page it had:

Thursday 7 June   Today's Reading John 3:16

GOD'S PROVISION TO THE WORLD

Then half-way down the page I read

> For God so loved the world that He gave His one and only Son. Jesus paid the full price for *our* freedom from sin. He was slaughtered like a lamb, a guiltless sacrifice, the propitiation for us. This was no small thing. If Jesus had not died for us, we would never be able to communicate with God, we would only have eternal damnation to look forward to. We would be for ever lost.

My heart was doing somersaults, causing the rest of my body to vibrate. I could even feel the blood rushing in my ears. I wanted to get off the bus. Fresh air was what I needed.

'Are you okay?'

I looked at the woman.

'What's wrong?'

I gulped.

'Do you feel sick or something?'

I nodded.

'I'll get the conductor to stop the bus.'

She began to put her book away.

I touched her arm to stop her. 'No, I'm all right.'

Looking at me intently, she said, 'You don't look all right. Look, can I help you?'

'Well, I, eh . . . '

86

She could see that I was having difficulty speaking.
'What's your name?'
'Jas.'
'That's short for Jasmine.' She smiled.
I smiled back. Feeling a little calmer, I asked her what her name was.
'Simone. Simone Campbell.'
'Are you a Christian?' I could have bitten my tongue.
She beamed at me. 'Why, yes. Are you?'
'That's a good question.'
Taking a deep breath, I launched into a lengthy conversation about the dream, the posters, the Fentons, Aszal, and my mum being in hospital. Afterwards I rested back in my seat, worn out and a bit dazed. How I had managed to confide all my troubles to a complete stranger I don't know. Simone was a good listener, I'll give her that. She didn't interrupt me once, she just let me get it all out. It left me with a good feeling.
'What an exciting life,' she said.
'Exciting? You must be crazy. The only exciting thing for me is the band that I'm in. I'm into rap music.'
'That's what most young people are into these days. I would have been surprised if you had said that you liked classical music.'
'You must be crazy.' I laughed out loud.
We sat quietly for a few moments, then Simone spoke. 'Now, I know you may think this is corny and that I'm as nutty as the Fentons, but I really believe that God had planned for us to meet. This bus isn't the one I usually get, I get the one after.'
'Funny you should say that,' I spluttered out. 'I should have got the one before.'
'There. You see?'
'Oh yeah. That was just luck.'
'You think so? What is luck?'
'It's when things go your way. And when things don't, it's unlucky.'

'But that's leaving things to chance. Wouldn't you like to have a bit more control over your life? It won't be half as puzzling.'

'Don't tell me — become a Christian.'

'You said it.'

'What I can't understand is, why do these Christians think they know all about God? So do Muslims and everybody else who believes in God. Surely as long as you believe you'll be all right.'

'If only it were that easy. As far as we Christians are concerned, there is only one God, and Jesus Christ is His Son. That's where a lot of people go wrong, they don't believe that Jesus is God's Son. He is the only way to God.'

'Well, I can't see what the problem is. I believe in Jesus.'

'Ha, now we're coming on to some meaty stuff.'

Simone got comfortable in her seat and turned to me as though she was going to divulge some top secret: 'Many people believe in Jesus, the Muslims do and lots of other religions, but they don't want to commit their lives to Him, com-plete-ly.'

The way she said completely made me want to laugh — it was like she had a wine gum in her mouth.

'What do you mean completely?'

'Completely means saying to God, "Okay Lord, I'm no longer going to live my life for myself and do the things I want to do, but I'm going to live for You, according to how You stated in Your Word that I should." For example, if, say, when you get home, Judy, Mrs Fenton, is very upset that you are late and you get a telling off — '

"Don't remind me."

'Well, you could react how any young person would and give her a mouthful back, or you could try and explain why you were late and, if that didn't work, say nothing at all, just an apology.'

'You are crazy. There is no way that I would let Judy think she had the upper hand. I'll really give it to her, in fact that is just what I'm waiting for. She won't know what's hit her.'

Simone sat back, folding her arms. 'That's just what I mean. Listen, how do you think Jesus would have reacted?'

Thinking I was being very clever, I piped up, 'He would have turned the other cheek.'

'Good girl, you're spot on.'

'But Simone, this is the 1990s. Communism looks like it's on the way out, microchips are here to stay, safe sex doesn't stop Aids and rap music is going to reign, and you're trying to tell me that you must let some ignorant person walk all over you. No wonder churches are empty. Eye for an eye, tooth for a tooth, that's what I'm into.'

'Live by the sword, die by the sword. We all have a free will; how we choose to live is entirely up to us. God doesn't force anyone − it's a love relationship. Choose today life or death.'

For a moment she looked at me sadly as though she was going to cry. I looked out of the window hoping she wouldn't become all emotional.

'Oh, look, it's my stop. Here, take my number, ring me any time, and I'll be praying for your mum for tomorrow.' She shoved a scrap of paper into my hand and leapt up, then bent over and quickly pecked me on the cheek. 'Bye, Jas. God bless you.'

Waving to Simone who was still standing at the bus stop, I felt empty inside, just like after you've eaten everything in sight, yet still you aren't satisfied. I breathed deeply and thought back over the day. It was strange, meeting Robert and then Simone. I must admit, she had made some sort of sense about Jesus, though I still couldn't see what it was all about. Trying to piece things together I came up with a heavy duty question: if there were such places as Heaven and Hell, did that mean that non-believers and all the people who belonged to other religious groups and even people who did believe in Jesus but didn't give their lives or souls to Him − that all these people were going to Hell? Surely not. If God loves the world so much, no one should be going to Hell. But that didn't sound too right even to me — what about murderers and child molesters and criminals of all descriptions and basically vile, wicked people of whom I could right now name a few? Hmm.

This was no easy question, and I wasn't really bothered, but I could feel a gnawing at the back of my brain. What is the answer?

The bus pulled into Romford. As I was stepping off the bus I decided that I didn't want to go to Hell (if there was such a place) but this church business was not for me.

There was standing room only on the bus to Upminster. The time was 5.40. Judy would be having a litter of kittens by now. Thinking about how she was going to explode like an atomic bomb when I got home, I soon forgot about the eternal Hell, and dreaded the living one I would be walking into soon.

10

If there was ever a day in my life that I wished hadn't happened, it was that Friday. It could have been Friday the thirteenth for all the unfortunate episodes that occurred.

To give credit where it's due, it really started when I came home late from school on Thursday. Judy was having more than kittens, she was having a fold of sheep too! She was like a raving lunatic. Even her eyes were red!

It's not easy trying to explain to someone on the verge of having a massive heart attack why you were late. (I blamed the buses. Admittedly it was chatting to Robert that had caused the delay, but I didn't offer that bit of information: what you don't know don't hurt you!) To top it off, when I muttered under my breath about the virtues of being a Christian (just what Simone had said: turn the other cheek and all that), Judy's eyes became steel-like and her lips went white.

Cana had skulked off upstairs by this time. I supposed she didn't want to witness murder. Matt was hanging around so I guessed that he did!

I really couldn't see what all the fuss was about. All right, so I was late. I had apologised, but obviously that wasn't enough. My blood was required too. Halfway through this mêlée Aubrey came in. Thank God.

He sent me to my room. I ran.

Cana was lying on her bed staring at the ceiling. She didn't budge an inch when I came in.

'Cana?'

91

She didn't acknowledge her name being called.

'Cana, what's wrong?

I thought for a moment she was going to say something but she didn't. I can't stand silences for too long so I spoke.

'I'm really sorry about being late. I have said it a million times to your mum, but it's like heaping more salt on an open wound. What I can't understand is why she's acting like a demented farm animal just because I'm late. What is the problem? I don't think there's anybody on this earth who has never been late, except perhaps Jesus — but I'm sure if somebody He was waiting for was late He wouldn't behave like your mother. Does she really dislike me so much?'

I flopped down on the edge of Cana's bed.

'No,' she replied.

'Well, put it this way: she has a funny way of showing me that she does like me.'

Cana rolled over on to her side, facing me. 'My mother has a few problems, much like the rest of us.'

'That's putting it mildly.'

'You know, I've sat and thought about my mum whenever she goes off the edge like this and I've come to the conclusion that it is either because she's insecure, or just that she has a violent temper that she hasn't learnt to control. I think it's probably the latter. I really can't understand why she explodes like that. Most of the time she's great, very understanding, reasonable, but then there comes a time when — bang — she flips. She'll come and say she's sorry after she's calmed down.'

I laughed. 'Say sorry? I doubt it very much. So much for Christianity.'

'No, she will, I'm sure of it. And Jas, don't keep knocking Christianity just because my mum's upset — '

'That's putting it a bit soft — upset.'

'Yeah, well, she is very upset that you were late, and very worried. She gets like that with anyone who upsets her routine. But it doesn't mean that she isn't a Christian and she doesn't care about people, quite the opposite in fact. What you have to realise is that one is a human being first and then a Christian after. To be a Christian is to be Christ-like. It's difficult when you're faced with everyday situations and problems, but the main thing is to keep trying.'

'I'll tell you something, Cana. Your mum was very lucky that *I* didn't explode. While she was mouthing me off I had to control myself because I wanted to punch her right in her mouth and watch her teeth crumble. I know it sounds terrible but I did. Yet I controlled myself. So, as an adult, I can't see why *she* couldn't control *her*self.'

Sighing, Cana stood up. 'Okay. You and I know, Jas, that life hasn't been easy here for you. A strange family with strange ways, loss of privacy, your life has been turned upside down. But you haven't made it easier for yourself or us.'

'How do I make it easier for myself or for you lot, eh? The only solution that I can come up with is to leave.'

Swinging her legs over the side of the bed, Cana moved next to me. 'Listen Jas, leaving a difficult situation isn't necessarily the way to deal with it. Face it head on, clear the air and you may even surprise yourself. I've done that with my mum. We used to clash so much. I would even go as far as to say that I strongly disliked her. But I thought one day, what's the point? Let her have her say and it will blow over, and it did. So that's what I do.'

'Oh yeah, what about the other day? You were like a wild cat.'

'Hmm. That was different.'

'I see. Some — .'

'No, hold on. It's a question of trying. I try to contain myself, but I'm not always successful. How about you? You said that you controlled yourself today, and it worked. What if you had had a fight with Mum?' She rolled her eyes up to the ceiling.

'I'd have definitely been leaving, whether I wanted to or not,' I said grimly.

'There, see? Now you know what I'm talking about.'

Taking a deep breath, I went and lay on my bed. All this hassle about being late. Why didn't she pray that I wasn't in any trouble? Instead she saves up her anger to explode in my face.

I didn't want to go to school on Friday. The rest of Thursday evening I had spent in my room. Cana was right: Judy came up and apologised and we had spoken in quite a civilised way, but I still didn't trust her. Just before she went downstairs she gave me a bear hug and kissed my cheek. I felt embarrassed.

After she had gone, I tried to figure her out. The only people who hugged me like that were Mum, and definitely not after a heated argument, and Rosa who was the sort of child who liked to hug everyone. Sometimes she got on my nerves too! I thought that Judy had made that big show about apologising to me so that when I told Brenda she wouldn't look so bad. But somehow I knew that there was more to it. What, though?

I fell asleep trying to puzzle it out.

I didn't wake until the next morning, and that was because someone wanted me on the phone. I nearly broke my neck rushing downstairs to answer it. My foot got tangled up in my dressing-gown belt.

'Hello, Jas speaking . . . Oh no . . . Okay . . . Can I see her today? . . . Fine. Bye.'

Judy popped her head round the kitchen door. 'Everything all right, Jas?'

'No.'

'Do you want to talk about it?'

I looked at her, thinking she's a right Jekyll and Hyde character. She seemed so concerned about me. But I told her all the same. 'My mum's not having her operation today, something about not having her blood type in the bank. She's to have the operation some time next week.'

Judy tutted. 'Not to worry. You can go and see her tonight.' She hesitated.

'It's okay, I'll tell you before I do, so that you know whether to expect me or not.'

'That's very thoughtful of you, Jas.' She smiled.

I didn't smile back. That's all she wants: people doing what she wants.

'Oh, Jas,' Judy called as I made my way back upstairs. 'Remember that Aszal and his family are coming round tonight, and Aunt Myrtle is coming home this afternoon.'

'Okay.'

I had forgotten. My brain began to churn over. How can I go and see Mum tonight and still be here when Aszal comes? The solution was easy: don't go to school. So I didn't.

I dropped in on Brenda at her office and then I went to see Mum. I spent most of the day with her. It was great. Brenda had sorted out my absence from school with the headmistress, which was cool. I asked her to talk to Judy too, as I didn't want a repeat of the day before.

After I had visited Mum, I decided on the spur of the moment to go and see Donelle and Rosa too.

I arrived outside the school gates in time to see Rosa leaping into Donelle's outstretched arms.

'Hi Rosa, hi Donelle,' I shouted.

'Jas, Jas,' they both screamed.

People were turning round to look at us. I didn't give a monkey's.

They both looked really well and healthy.

'What's Aunt Merri's cooking like?'

Rosa turned up her nose.

Donelle said, 'Rice, rice and more rice. She doesn't believe in baked beans and sausages, and as for chips . . . ' She giggled.

Kissing and hugging them both made me feel alive and good. I hadn't realised how much I had missed them.

Aunt Merri turned up from nowhere. 'Shouldn't you be at school young lady?'

Glaring at her, I said, 'Hello, Aunt Merri.' Even though she hadn't said it to me. I knew that she would moan if I didn't say hello first.

'You haven't answered my question. Well, child?'

'Brenda, Mum's social worker, had to see me, which meant I had to have the day off from school. I've just come from visiting Mum, so I thought I'd come and see the girls too.'

'You coming home with us, Jas?' enquired Rosa.

I looked at Aunt Merri. If it was left to me, I would be going with them, whether she wanted me to or not.

She could see me looking at her, ready to defy her. She said yes.

Aunt Merri's house was about ten minutes away from the school by car, but the way she drove it was more like twenty. If you had to choose one word to sum up her house, it would have to be 'spotless'. Not a speck anywhere. I wondered how the girls had managed to keep it clean and tidy.

'Don't hang your jacket on the banisters, Jasmine. Put it in the cupboard under the stairs.'

She was like that with everything. I was getting a headache.

The girls were a little subdued while we were in Aunt Merri's company, but once we got up to their room, it was bedlam. They threw themselves on the bed, on the floor, screaming and laughing. I was in the thick of it too — well, I couldn't be a spoilsport.

There was a knock at the door followed by Aunt Merri's voice and then her head: 'That's enough excitement for one day. Calm down, girls. Dinner will soon be ready.'

Breathless we sat on the bed. Rosa was kissing and hugging me all the time. I wanted her to stop — it was annoying me a bit — but I knew that she would get upset, so I left her slobbering all over me.

'How's Mum?' asked Donelle.

'Fine. She's not having her operation today, next week sometime.'

'When we will be able to see Mum and go home, Jas?'

I shrugged my shoulders. 'Soon, I hope.'

'What's the family like you're living with?'

For one moment I forgot who she was referring to. Then I remembered.

'Oh, them. Okay, I suppose. But I'd rather be home with you two, even if you do drive me mad.'

'You drive us mad, too. Doesn't she, Rosa?'

Rosa just grinned up at me.

'I've got a new dolly, Jas.' Rosa held up a chocolate-coloured doll.

'Where did you get that from?'

Donelle answered. 'Aunt Merri's got a man friend who brought it for us. He goes to her church.'

'It's her boyfriend,' giggled Rosa.

I gasped. It couldn't be possible. Was there really a human being in the world who liked Aunt Merri?

'He has a thick beard and a big big belly, and you can't see his eyes through his glasses.'

Laughter erupted loudly out of my mouth. I could see why he liked her, he couldn't see properly, poor man. If only he could, he would run a mile!

Aunt Merri knocked and came into the room, offering me dinner. I refused, partly because of what Donelle told me about Aunt Merri's dishes and partly because of the tea party that awaited me when I got back to the Fentons.

Saying goodbye to the girls made me wish I hadn't come. Rosa was clinging on to me for dear life and Donelle looked tearful.

Aunt Merri took me aside and said: 'Would you please notify me before you come again? Then I can get the girls ready for you. Now look how upset they are.'

I felt guilty. Poor darlings. Disentangling myself from them again I promised I would see them next week.

*

97

I got home for 4.30. Judy was in the kitchen. I started to explain why I was home so early, as usually I would still be on the bus, but she already knew. Brenda had contacted her.

'Thanks for telling me anyway.' She patted my shoulder. 'Go and say hello to Aunt Myrtle. She's in the front room.'

I could hear Matt laughing his head off, and Aunt Myrtle's voice: ' . . . "But nurse, how can yu treat dat woman soo bad? Yu nar have no feeling. De poor ole woman. Yu know nurse yu need Jesus. Yes mi dear, yu really need a dose of de Holy Spirit." And yu know what Matt? De stupid nurse ask me if de Holy Spirit is a type of rum.' She kissed her teeth.

When I pushed open the door Matt was rolling all over the floor and I was grinning.

'Hi Aunt Myrtle.'

'Hello mi dear. Judy did tell mi sey yu is still here, dat's nice. Come, come and give auntie a kiss.'

I obeyed dutifully.

'Yu Christian yet?'

I nodded, then shook my head. She had put me on the spot. I wasn't sure what to answer, which was stupid because I knew that the sort of Christianity that she meant wasn't my idea of it at all. Anyway Matt answered for me.

'No, Aunt Myrtle. She's resisting Jesus instead of the devil.'

'Well, never mind. Mi is here now. All de help and encouragement yu need, is mi will guide yu.'

She was reclining on the sofa, fully clothed with a quilted dressing gown on top and a thick blanket covering her legs. I wondered if she was that cold! Next to her was a side table laden with books, a jug of water, a box of chocolates and various bits and pieces.

'Mi know sey mi going to enjoy miself here, with so much young people inna de house too.'

I grinned weakly and backed out of the door.

Flying up the stairs I thought it might not be so good after all having Aunt Myrtle staying in the house. She was very forceful, making it difficult to answer her back. A bit like Aunt Merri. As for that cheeky Matt, telling her that I was following the devil — he should talk!

Lying on the bed with my headphones on I was beginning to feel concerned that since I had been in this house I was finding it very hard to write lyrics. If we wanted to be serious as a band we needed new material all the time. I tried very hard to concentrate, but it was like trying to get water out of a dry tap! Nothing.

I must have dozed off because the next thing I knew, Cana was tugging my arm quite violently.

'Wake up Jas, wake up. Everybody's here.'

'What, what?'

'Come on, Aszal and his mum and his brother Tukah are here. The table's set, we are only waiting for you.'

I sprang out of bed like an Olympic hurdler. I was in and out the bathroom and dressed in about five minutes flat. Breathlessly I brushed my hair.

'Do I look all right, Cana?'

She grinned at me. 'You look the same to me.'

'Thanks very much for your detailed answer, Cana. Remind me not to ask for your opinion in future.'

As I followed Cana downstairs I began to get nervous, wondering how Aszal would be towards me. I wasn't too pleased that his mum was here. From the impression that I got at the church she wasn't the sort of person that you could be friendly with. She was cold. And I also thought about the way he was with his mum, handling her as though she were made of gold. Oh well, I thought, it's not his mum that I'm interested in.

When we entered the lounge everyone was seated at the table. There were two empty chairs, one between Matt and Aszal's brother and the other between Aszal and Aunt Myrtle. I didn't know which one to choose. I would have loved to just stroll up all casual-like and sit next to Aszal but I just couldn't do it. Anyway, the need to decide was taken away from me: Cana sat next to Matt.

I was very uncomfortable sitting next to Aszal. I wished I had sat across the table from him — eye contact I can handle.

I must have been totally blinded by Aszal because I didn't realise at first that there was somebody extra at the table who I didn't even know. Judy introduced us.

'Jas, this is Hina. Hina, this is Jas.'

'Hello.'

'Hi.'

Hina was sort of pretty. She had waist-length light brown hair, a small button nose and thickish lips, but somehow her lips didn't look out of place on her face. She seemed the quiet and timid sort. She was small and bony — underdeveloped from what I could see. Aszal and his mother who were sitting on either side of her dwarfed her.

Aszal piped up: 'Hina means goose in Greek. Hina's a little goose.' He smiled at me, then turned and smiled at her. She smiled at him and then looked down at her plate.

What's going on here? Her looking at him like a right goose (I could see why she was called that) and him looking sheepishly at her. I felt sick.

All through tea Aunt Myrtle dominated the conversation, which was great as I didn't have too much to say.

I wanted to find out what 'little goosey goosey gander' meant to Aszal. Thinking for a moment 'why am I bothering' and not being able to answer confused me all the more. Did I really like him a lot and not want to admit it even to myself? I wasn't sure. But I still wanted to know what Hina meant to him.

After the meal Cana, Hina, Aszal and I went up to Cana's room. Everyone apart from Hina joined in the conversation which was all about love. No, not the smoochy kind, the Jesus kind. I surprised even myself by talking freely. I have only a limited knowledge of the subject after all.

Whenever Aszal said something like 'anyone can have this

100

love, it's free, it's fulfilling, it's the highest form of love', I swear he was looking at me. He certainly wasn't looking at Hina. She kept her eyes on her fingernails and only occasionally looked up at us, or more to the point, Aszal. I could see very plainly that she fancied Aszal. He didn't seem too bothered. It was a nice atmosphere, I felt relaxed.

Trust Cana to steer the topic round to marriage. Funnily enough, Aszal sort of clamped up and only muttered a few words. Cana gave a kind of lecture or more like a one-sided conversation. I didn't have much to add, not knowing much about marriage.

As Cana droned on and on Hina started talking. She was like a runaway train; starting off with a few sentences here and there, she soon began to zoom away. Cana shut up.

' — I think marriage is very special. It's a union between a man and a woman and God.'

I wondered what God had to do with it. Then again, I suppose He has because people get married in church.

'. . . It is God who puts couples together. Unlike in the world when people are physically attracted to someone of the opposite sex and decide to get married, but not for the right reasons. A marriage that is brought about by divine intervention must last for ever and ever.'

My tongue was paralysed. Never would I have believed that Goosey had so much chat in her mouth! I don't think she even stopped for breath. The amazing thing was that while she was rabbiting on nobody interrupted her: Cana nodded now and again and Aszal just kept his head down. I think he felt embarrassed.

After Hina finished, or dried up, Cana asked if anyone wanted something to drink.

'Tea please, one sugar,' Aszal said.

Hina jumped up so quickly she was like a cannon fired from a rocket. 'I'll make it.'

'Okay,' said Cana. 'What do you want, Jas?'

'Eh, coffee, I think. Black no sugar.'

'You're very good, no milk or sugar,' grinned Aszal.

101

I was so caught up with his smiling face and twinkling eyes that I didn't answer him at first.

Cana stepped in. 'Ask her about chocolate and you'll get a different picture, Aszal.'

I lowered my eyes, I couldn't face him.

'What's all this about Jas? You have a passion for chocolate?'

The way he said passion made me feel so stupid, no words could come out of my mouth.

'Come on, Hina, let's make the drinks.'

Aszal and I were left alone. He got up from his position on the floor and walked over to the window.

'How's life, Jas?' He turned to look at me.

Shrugging, I said it was fine.

'No more nightmares?'

I shook my head.

'That's good, I was quite concerned about you. I've been asking Cana and Matt how you are when I've seen or spoken on the phone to them.'

I began to feel sweaty and hot. This guy was more or less telling me that he felt something for me. Why else would he be enquiring about my wellbeing?

'That's nice of you to be concerned.'

He looked at me and then back out of the window. He didn't answer. The deafening silence was becoming unbearable. I was really trying hard to think of something to say when Cana and Hina came back.

'Drinks up, folks,' said Cana merrily.

Sipping our drinks, we just talked about nothing in particular. Time slipped by quickly.

Judy came into the room. 'Everything all right? Your mother's ready to leave, Aszal.'

'Okay.'

We all trooped downstairs.

In the lounge Aubrey suggested that we link hands and pray. My hand fitted Aszal's hand perfectly, like a made-to-measure glove. I didn't hear a word of Aubrey's prayer.

102

My mind was just taken up with Aszal holding my hand. Is this love?

All too soon Aubrey finished and we were waving goodbye to them at the front door. Judy put her arm around my shoulder.

'Have a nice time, Jas?'

I was surprised at her: at that moment she seemed soft and gentle.

'Yeah, I did, as a matter of fact.'

'I'm glad. We will do it again soon.'

I knew that once we were in bed Cana would question me about Aszal. I was right.

'Well, what did you talk about whilst we were out of the room?'

'Nothing.'

'Oh come on, Jas. What did he say to you?'

'Nothing. I think he was choked up.'

'You've fallen for him, haven't you?'

'No,' I denied hotly and a bit too quickly.

'All I can say is be careful. Aszal has all the girls chasing him and sometimes I think he can't handle it.'

Going off the subject a bit, I asked Cana if I should invite Aszal to the rap competition.

'You can only ask.'

The last picture in my head as I snuggled under the duvet was of me blasting out some mega-lyrics, feeling proud, while Aszal looked on with shining face, bright eyes fixed on me alone.

Yeah. I'm inviting him.

11

'Salvation is life. Now yu might not agree wid mi, but chile, mi can tell yu dat dere is nuttin else in dis life except de Lawd. Yu can drink, but yu nar happy, yu can have bwoyfriend to kiss and sex yu, but yu nar have peace of mind. All de money and riches yu can have, nar buy yu long life or love. Only de Lawd Jesus can supply all yu need and more.' Aunt Myrtle popped a peppermint into her mouth and coughed.

Propped up in bed she looked like a miniature doll. I had slipped into Aunt Myrtle's room while everyone was busy doing something. I was dying to have a chat with her.

'But Aunt Myrtle, I believe in Jesus and God, but I don't feel it's necessary to do a song and dance about it and tell the whole world.'

She looked at me for a while and then said: 'When yu love somebody, all yu talk bout is yur bwoyfriend. Yu dream bout him, and when yu not talking bout him to anybody dat will listen, yu a daydream bout him. Every minute yur mind full of de bwoyfriend. Is de same way when yu is a Christian. God spirit full yu up wid love and all yu want to do is talk bout Him. It more den belief. Much more.'

I thought about what she said. Going by the experience with Aszal (which I knew was only in the early days), I could understand what Aunt Myrtle meant.

I was kneeling at the side of Aunt Myrtle's bed. The Saturday morning sun gently nosed its way through the window. It warmed my body, and the thought of Aszal warmed me inside. I wanted to confide in Aunt Myrtle about Aszal, but something told me not to, or not yet. Before breakfast I had wanted to talk about him to Cana. I was dying to know about Hina, but I just couldn't bring myself to ask. I'd hoped Cana would volunteer information, but she hadn't.

Lisa had phoned me after breakfast, but I wasn't able to have a long chat with her. The telephone is in the hall and even though I could have plugged it into the living room, people were always walking about. I didn't want to be overheard.

'. . . Nobody can be forced to come to Jesus. Yu have to have a desire.'

I was only half listening to Aunt Myrtle. It was crazy. I had never felt this way before towards any boy. I had tried to reason out what was happening to me. It was difficult. If only I could talk to someone who could throw some light on to the matter. But who?

Turning round to sit on the floor, I came face to face with the posters. A chill went down my spine.

'Aunt Myrtle, I had a nightmare last week, and it keeps coming back to me.'

'What de nightmare?'

'No, I don't keep having the nightmare, but what the nightmare was about keeps coming back to me.'

'So what is de nightmare bout, eh?'

Taking a deep breath I related the nightmare from beginning to end. Aunt Myrtle never spoke a word. As I was finishing off I felt uneasy. Aunt Myrtle was sitting very still as though she was listening out for something. I had stopped speaking, but she didn't start.

'Aunt Myrtle?' I sat up.

She looked at me. A feeling of dread passed through my body like the senna tea that Mum insists we take at the beginning of every school holiday.

Breathing in, Aunt Myrtle began to speak: 'De dream is very plain to mi. Jesus is calling yu.'

I waited for her to say something more but she didn't. She just stared at me, which made me feel more uneasy than if she had spoken.

'Well, hmm, I don't really, I hmm.'

'Chile. It is a big decision. De biggest decision yu will ever make in yur whole life. Yu must take time and consider. Once yu commit yur life to Jesus dere is no turning — ' she waved her hand in the air, 'no turning back. Yu know, it is worse if yu give yur life to Jesus and turn back. God nar like backslider — '

'Backslider, what's that?' I asked.

'Just like mi said, someone who start off life with de Lawd and turn back, but if yu turn back again, Him still accept yu. What a wonderful Saviour.' She leant back against the pillows with her arms folded and her eyes closed. I thought that it was an opportune moment to sneak out. I was mistaken.

As I stood up, Aunt Myrtle's eyes flew open, and so did her mouth.

'Is where yu going?'

Guiltily I looked down at the floor (just like Rosa when she has done something wrong and you have caught her). My eyes couldn't meet Aunt Myrtle's.

'I, eh . . . '

'Come sit down. We nar finish talk yet.'

Obediently I sat back on the floor.

'Now, is today yu will choose life or death.'

I really didn't want to hear this.

'Imagine dat Almighty God sent His Son Jesus, to die for yu and me.' She pointed her finger at me and then herself. 'Would yu die in place of somebody else?'

'That's a silly thing to ask. Of course not.'

'Hmm. So if somebody do it fi yu, yu must tank dem.'

'If I had committed some crime or other, yes, but I haven't done anything yet,' I replied indignantly.

Aunt Myrtle laughed. 'Oh, so yu is sin-free.'

I shrugged. What Aunt Myrtle had said seemed familiar.

Where had I had this conversation before? I couldn't remember.

'Well, mi chile, is not always dat God's Spirit contend with flesh. Him will leave yu to yur own device, and take it from mi, yu will suffer.'

Simone. My heart began to thud wildly. I couldn't believe it — I had had an identical conversation with Simone on the bus. Is God really everywhere? Does He listen in to every conversation? This is freaky, I thought. I wished that I was at home with Mum and the girls. Life was hassle-free, without maniacs trying to force religion down my throat. I was choking from an overdose.

I wanted to change the subject but I couldn't come up with anything.

Aunt Myrtle did it for me:

'How is yur mudda?'

Phew! Thank God for that.

'Eh, she's all right. She was supposed to have her operation yesterday, but it's been put off until next week.'

'Poor ting. Mi a pray fi her. God will take care, He is de great Physician in de sky.'

Laughter bubbled up inside me at the thought of God's hand coming out of the sky and doing Mum's operation. Honestly, I could let Aunt Myrtle off for saying something so bizarre. After all she was an old woman.

Aunt Myrtle asked me about Dad and the girls and we talked about things in general.

I asked her about her family and it was like discovering an oil well. She gushed forth a stream of words and accompanying gestures. She must have talked for about an hour. When I got the chance, I brought up Judy's name. I was dying to find out what she felt about her and whether she liked her or not.

'Mi must tell de truth and sey dat from de time mi see de white skin, mi tink sey nuttin good going to come of dis. Mi good good nephew who work so hard a college, sacrifice himself a study fi exam and pass wid no problem, den, pick

107

a white woman! Even if she was Indian gal mi could take it but, blonde hair — ' She turned her nose up.

'Just what I thought. Couldn't Aubrey have found a nice black woman who was just as intelligent, and she could have still been a Christian? Most black people are Christians from what I can gather. She must have done something to him, or for him.' I looked knowingly at Aunt Myrtle. 'It must have been all that studying that turned his brain.'

'What yu seying chile?'

The way she said it made me pause before I answered.

'Well, I, hmm, find it strange that he is so handsome and he ended up with — '

'No, yu is wrong, chile. God put de two of dem togedder. Whom God put togedder let no man put asunder. After mi consider de fact dat Aubrey nar fool. Him love Jesus, him could not take on de big responsibility of choosing him own wife. Him leave dat decision up to de Lawd.'

I was shocked that even Aunt Myrtle agreed that it should be God that chose your husband or your wife — what if you didn't like them?

'And yu know, Judy is really an angel. Yu know she come in like mi daughter, if mi did have one. She have manners, she bring up de picknee beau-ti-fully. Mis is so proud she is mi niece. Dis colour problem is a lie from de devil. God made Adam and Eve. Everybody' — she threw her arms wide, into the air — 'come from dem. No matter what colour yu is we all one family.'

Aunt Myrtle had to be kidding. Or was this senile dementia?

To throw a spanner in the works I put a question to her: 'What about the National Front and the Nazis and anybody else who hates other people of a different race to them, how do you account for that?'

'Oh chile, when yu reach as ole as mi, yu will realise dat de world is full of wicked people. How can yu hate somebody yu nar know? Is mad. Yu must be mad. Dem people just full of evil spirit. Tank de Lawd, because if dem nar change dem ways, hmm, de Lawd will deal wid dem. Nar worry yurself.'

Thoughts of Aunt Myrtle liking Judy revolved in my head. I was surprised to hear her say such things about her. So much for thinking I'd have an ally in Aunt Myrtle.

'Jas,' Judy called from downstairs.

'Go see what Judy want, chile.'

As I was getting up to go, she added: 'Jasmine, remember yu have a big decision to make.' Then, snuggling under the duvet, she dismissed me.

Judy was putting her jacket on as I got to the bottom of the stairs.

'Jas, Cana and I are going shopping. Do you want to come?'

'No, it's okay. I've got things to do.'

'You sure?'

I nodded. There was no way that I wanted to go out with her and Cana. The two of them together must be a nightmare, besides I had a lot to think about.

'I'm just going to have a word with your father, Cana. I won't be a minute.' Judy trotted up the stairs.

'You sure you don't want to come, Jas?' Cana asked. 'It may be a chance for you to get to know Mum a bit more. Besides, she's quite generous with money, you might even get a little prezzie.'

'No thanks, I'm going to be very busy. I've hardly written any lyrics since I've been here and I must try and get something down on paper.'

I decided to raid the kitchen. When I passed Aubrey and Judy's bedroom with a glass of orange juice in one hand and a plate of biscuits in the other (I was planning to stuff myself), the door was slightly ajar and I could see them embracing. At first I wanted to get into my room quickly and not have to witness their sloppiness, but then I slowed down and watched them.

Both Aubrey's arms were around Judy and hers were intertwined around his neck. They were looking deeply into each other's eyes. That was it — they were just staring at each other. It was funny looking at them. I got the same feeling as I did when in Aszal's company. They must love each other then. Hmm. It still seemed strange to me. How could Aubrey love Judy? She was so miserable!

I was eager to go to church on Sunday morning. I knew it wasn't because of anything religious — I had been in the house all Saturday, which was quite unusual for me. At home I'm out all day on Saturdays with my friends: going to different markets (ending up at Walthamstow), sitting in McDonald's until we are thrown out or at someone's house, usually Lisa's — her mum's cool. So staying at home was 'way out' for me, to say the least.

Church was exactly the same. I wondered if people saved up all their energy during the week so that they could go mad on Sunday!

When church was over Hina appeared out of nowhere in front of us, followed by Aszal's mum. Aszal's mum didn't speak to me, just nodded her head, but she spoke to Judy. Hina said hello and then looked down at the floor. I wondered where Aszal was.

The talk about Judy with Aunt Myrtle the day before had made me re-evaluate the situation between Aszal and me as regards colour. As far as I was concerned, Aunt Myrtle would have been the last person to agree with mixed marriages.

Seeing Aubrey and Judy together, I'd had to admit reluctantly that there was something between them. That must sound strange, because after all they are married, but Mum says that even though some people are married for years, they don't love each other and only stick it out for one reason or another. So if Aubrey and Judy only tolerated each other, that I could have understood. But I'm not blind. I could see there was something more. Love is unpredictable.

Whenever I see an odd couple, like a fat woman and a skinny man or a tall man and a short woman, it makes me

110

laugh. But when I see a black and white couple I don't laugh:
I've always thought it was wrong.

Now I asked myself what I was going to think if the
situation with Aszal developed into a full-blown relationship.
I wouldn't be able to laugh because I was in it. Would I
think it was wrong? Of course not.

Growing older certainly made you think that life was a
labyrinth. Things seemed to overlap, nothing went in a
straight line. It seemed unbelievable that I might become
involved in the very thing I condemned.

It seemed that Aszal hadn't come to church at all. I must
admit that was the biggest reason why I was eager to get
there — just to see him.

Matt and Aszal's brother Tukah were chatting outside.
It was on the tip of my tongue to ask where Aszal was, but
I knew that if I did, Matt, being quick off the mark, would
want to know why I was interested, and put two and two
together. I left it. But I couldn't get it out of my mind.

Where was he? And why was Hina with his mum? Did
his mother see Hina as a prospective daughter-in-law?

We'll see about that.

111

12

Where does time go? I could hardly believe that I had been with the Fentons for four weeks and was still sane!

Cana and I had grown closer together. Our relationship was quite nice really. I didn't confide too much of my business to her — after all she is her mother's daughter — but we could talk about most things to each other. On a list of popularity of topics of conversation, boys would be number one. Discussing it with her made me feel that she was 'normal' too!

The only thing that caused a bit of friction between us was Aszal. I had decided to say as much as I thought needed to be said about him, but whenever I did, Cana was very unresponsive. Like the time I asked her about Hina: she didn't want to say anything.

'Cana, come on. Tell me what you know about Hina the goose.'

She tutted.

'I know you know something but you're not telling me. Why? Are you so loyal to Aszal that you can't tell me? Come on, what's the mystery?'

'There is no mystery. You can see that she obviously likes Aszal — '

'Likes him!' I laughed. 'She's obsessed. Not a healthy sign. That's why people commit "Crimes of Passion": they can't distinguish between love and obsession. But what's more important to me is how do you think Aszal feels about her?'

112

'I don't know.'

'Yes you do. Come on, out with it.'

'Let's change the subject shall we?'

That's how far we usually got.

I knew that Aszal liked me. I would go even so far as to say that I felt that it was more than liking me, but I thought it was better to be cool and wait, than to be hot and in a hurry. I was dying to ask him to come to the rap competition, but somehow I just couldn't get the words out!

I eventually plucked up courage. I was sitting next to him during the church youth meeting (I went to be near him — a bit corny I know, but it was the only way) and I asked him if he wanted to come to my next gig which was the competition.

He said YES! No hesitation. No 'I'll let you know later'. No 'I can't make it'. Just plain yes. I could have screamed. I couldn't sleep that night.

Since then I had been working the girls so hard, getting the act polished and together. I wanted to make a good impression as well as win the competition.

Life with Matt hadn't changed. He was still the same pain in the neck. I was so glad that I hadn't a brother, because if he was anything like Matt, I would have killed him long ago. He found any excuse to tease and play jokes on me and Cana. Aubrey seemed to think it was funny too, and encouraged him, to make matters worse!

Cana and I started to devise our own little schemes to get back at them. Like the time they played that old trick, putting a bag of flour on the top of our door: we open the door and, you've guessed it, we're covered in flour. Judy wasn't very pleased. Matt made an attempt to Hoover it up, but in the end it was Cana and I who had to clean it off the carpet. So we played a trick back on him: emptying the bottle of tomato ketchup into Matt's football boots. He didn't discover it until he was in the changing rooms ready

113

to go on the pitch — he was fuming when he got home. It was all great fun.

Practical jokes were something I had never really done before. I quite enjoyed myself.

Judy still remained an enigma. She seemed nice enough, but — and it was a big but — I felt that underneath something was brewing. I thought at first that I was making it all up — you know, paranoia. But sometimes you can feel something so strongly that it's almost real, and yet you can't see it — it isn't real.

As Mum would say, time will tell.

One thing I was very grateful for — and to give credit where it's due — staying at the Fentons while Mum was in hospital was a sure buffer against the acute anxiety that I went through.

Mum had the operation the Wednesday after the Friday that it was put off. The hospital phoned me before school and the nurse informed me that it was going to be today.

I couldn't go to school. Judy offered to stay at home with me but even though I was grateful for the offer I didn't fancy spending all day with her.

Instead I sat up in Aunt Myrtle's room. As usual, she was wrapped up to the hilt, with only her face and hands exposed, even though it wasn't cold. How she wasn't roasting to death I don't know!

We had a fantastic time together — she was marvellous. I found out just how funny she was. She has such a dry sense of humour and was cracking me up with her tales about her life in Jamaica when she was a young girl.

' . . . living in de yard was dangerous. Everybody know everybody business. Times when mi shoulda been in church we out a sport man. But mi never tell mi mudda odderwise she woulda kill mi dead. But Mabel Francis, one big mout gal, did see mi out with Georgie and run go tell mi mudda. When mi mudda catch mi, she give mi some licks mi could not sit down for de rest of de year. But, hmm, when mi catch

114

up with Mabel Francis, mi give her such a beating, all now she must still be fretting!'

Peals of outrageous laughter which I couldn't contain thundered around the room. I'm sure the people in the next road could hear! From what Aunt Myrtle told me I think it was a good thing that she became a Christian: otherwise, she would still be doing time for murder or something!

I phoned the hospital every hour but it nearly drove me nuts. All they said for the first few hours was that Mum was still in the operating theatre. When she finally came out, for the next couple of hours she was unconscious: 'No point in visiting, love, until she regains consciousness.'

When Aunt Myrtle suggested that we pray, I gladly fell on my knees. I just didn't know what else to do. Yet strangely enough I felt sort of all right while I was on my knees. I didn't know what to say, especially out loud, so in my mind I just asked God: As I'm a Christian (not in the sense that the Fentons are, but I do believe that You exist) and though You are obviously very busy – well, You have the whole world to look after – would You do me a favour and keep an eye on Mum for me and help her through the operation? I'm sure He was listening!

When Aunt Myrtle prayed I wanted to laugh (even though I knew it was out of place): 'Mi beg de Lawd pardon that mi can't knee down as yu know dat mi foot bruk!' But she prayed as though God was some bloke from down the street and that my mum was her best friend! It showed me that she cared and was a genuine person. From that time on I was consoled.

I got to see Mum that same evening. Aubrey and Judy came with me.

Mum was in a room of her own. The curtains were drawn and it felt as if time had stopped still in the room. The bed was raised at the bottom. Mum looked so small in the bed, surrounded by what seemed like all the pillows in the hospital. A bag of blood was hanging from a long pole and a red line ran from it into Mum's arm. I didn't want to look.

115

There was a big bunch of flowers on the bedside table. Being nosy, I read the label: 'To my darling wife, I miss you. Get better soon.' They were from Dad. I wanted to cry.

'Mum,' I whispered.

She moved in the bed. Judy gently pushed me close. No wonder Mum hadn't heard me: I was still standing at the door.

Leaning over her I called her again. This time she slowly opened her eyes.

'Hello, darling.'

Kissing her on her cheek, I said, 'How are you?'

'Tired.' She looked up at Aubrey and Judy. They all smiled at each other.

'How are you doing?' Aubrey asked.

'Fine.'

Aubrey and Judy took the chairs while I sat on the footstool. For most of the visit Mum slept, but I was just happy to be near her. I couldn't really say anything to her in front of the Fentons anyway.

The following Saturday I took the girls to see Mum. The way they jumped all over the bed, I was frightened they would split open her stitches.

Mum did brighten up, though. She laughed when Donelle (who would make a great policewoman when she grows up – asks hundreds of questions and is always snooping around) told her about Aunt Merri and her 'boyfriend', which was something Mum didn't know about.

'Aunt Merri told us we had to go to bed at seven o'clock instead of half seven because she was having a visitor and she didn't want us downstairs. But Mummy,' Donelle looked at Mum slyly, 'I couldn't sleep and I wanted a glass of water because I couldn't stop coughing, so I called for Aunt Merri. But she couldn't hear me so I went downstairs.' She stopped and looked at both Mum and me as though she was worried she could be in trouble if she said any more.

Mum's eyes were boring into Donelle's (danger signals),

116

but I'm sure she really wanted to know what her 'high moral standards' aunt was up to! She said: 'Go on.'

'Anyway, the living-room door happened to be open and Mr Cabbage Patch — '

'Who?' I burst out.

'Mr Cabbage Patch,' Rosa said. 'That's what we call Aunt Merri's boyfriend.'

Mum looked at Rosa, astonished.

'How does Rosa know him and why do you call him Mr Cabbage Patch?' she asked Donelle.

'Because,' Donelle said, taking a deep breath, 'Mr Cabbage Patch goes to church and afterwards he has dinner at Aunt Merri's, and he looks like Rosa's Cabbage Patch dolly.'

All very simple, I thought. On with the story.

' . . . Mr Cabbage Patch was doing up the back of Aunt Merri's dress.' Donelle folded her arms.

Mum looked as though she was lost for words. I was full of them but thought that this wasn't the best time to say anything.

'There was probably a good reason for Mr Cab — the gentleman to be fastening Aunt Merri's dress. Did you get your glass of water?'

'No. I wasn't thirsty any more.'

I would love to have been a fly on the wall in Aunt Merri's house. Adults complain about the young generation, that we're wild and 'footloose and fancy free' (Aunt Merri's own expression), when all the time it's them that are up to no good.

As we were about to leave the hospital, I asked: 'Mum, what would you say if I became a Christian like the Fentons?' I didn't mean to say it, but it just seemed to tumble out of my mouth. If someone had bet that I would ever say such a thing, I would have told them that they would lose their money.

'I would be very pleased, Jas,' Mum said. 'Before this operation, I promised God that if I came through it I would

117

go to church more often. God seems to have kept up his side of the agreement, so I'm keeping up mine.'

I groaned. This meant I would definitely have to go to church; Mum would expect me to go with her sometimes at least! Why couldn't I keep my big mouth shut?

The girls cried all the way back to Aunt Merri's. I told them that if this was how they were going to behave after visiting Mum I wouldn't take them in future. That was said outside Aunt Merri's gate, and it shut them up. I wished I had said it before!

I can understand why people go and see fortune-tellers — not that I really believe in that sort of stuff — but knowing about what the future holds must make you see or do things differently.

The week before the rap competition a placard should have been erected in the middle of the Fentons' front garden: NUCLEAR ZONE – DO NOT ENTER. If I had known what was going to happen I would have asked Brenda to take me away.

It was Friday night and Cana and I were at the youth meeting. I was sitting on the floor next to Cana with her friend Sara on the other side. Hina was facing me. Aszal hadn't turned up yet.

The subject matter was the tower of Babel. I had never heard of it before, so it was all new to me. Basically the story goes that God had created one nation, one language. Everyone spoke the same. But because of man's wickedness they all clubbed together to try to build a tower that went up to heaven so that they would make a name for themselves.

God apparently wasn't pleased. He said: 'If as one people speaking the same language they have begun to do this, then nothing they plan to do will be impossible for them.' So he confused their language so that they couldn't understand one another.

A nice fairy story, I thought. In fact I said it.

First there was silence and then the youth leader, Andy, kindly explained that: 'If it's in the Bible it's gospel.' At which some of the people twittered.

'So you're telling me that's how we got to speak in different languages. I would have thought that God would have come up with something more original, like, eh, I don't know . . .'

While all this was going on Aszal came in. As I was facing the door, he saw me first. I waved. He waved back and grinned. Hina turned round and saw him. She smiled at him and then glared back at me. She had obviously cottoned on that Aszal and I had exchanged greetings.

Someone was attempting to clarify the story when Hina piped up: 'The reason *some* people find it hard to believe is because the Spirit of God isn't in them, in fact the spirit in them comes from the pit.'

At first it didn't dawn on me that she could be speaking indirectly to me.

The room went quiet. I looked at Cana, then Sara, then Aszal. Aszal was the only one brave enough to look at me.

Then everyone started chatting at once.

'Excuse me. Hina, were you speaking to me?' I said loudly, pointing to myself.

She just looked.

'Well? I'm asking you a question.'

She looked at Aszal. Her eyes seemed to grow larger and they had that 'Little Bo-Peep has lost her sheep' expression.

'Hmm, well, sort of.'

'Sort of what do you mean?'

'It's, hmm, difficult to explain.'

'Is it really now? Well I've got the time, so speak.'

The room was deadly silent.

Hina took a deep breath, and looking me straight in the eye said: 'When you're not filled with the Holy Spirit, it causes problems for you in trying to understand God's word. It makes no sense. Therefore, if you haven't got the Spirit of God in you then you must have spirits from . . .'

'Having difficulty in putting it into words?' I enquired.

'Aszal, you explain about darkness and light.'

Looking steadily at Hina, Aszal never opened his mouth. But I did. 'Listen, Hina. You have got a problem. You fancy Aszal rotten, and you're jealous that he likes me, okay?'

Gasps and nervous giggles broke the silence.

'But let me tell you something. When a little toe-rag like you tries to insinuate that I have the devil in me, well, I think you are pushing things a little too far.' I stood up.

'So far in fact,' I said between clenched teeth as I walked over to her, 'that you deserve everything that you are going to get.'

Pow!

I slapped her face so hard I thought her head was going to turn round. She screamed. Looking over my shoulder, I said to Cana, 'I'm going now,' and left the room.

I was putting on my jacket which was hanging up on the end of the staircase when Andy, closely followed by Aszal, Cana and Sara, came out into the hall.

I was so angry I felt like I had a few evil spirits in me. My ears were red hot, my jaw was fixed tight – just like lockjaw – and my stomach was churning about like a high-powered washing machine.

Andy said: 'Jas, listen, I think you went a bit too far.'

Sara added: 'You shouldn't have hit Hina.'

Cana followed with: 'She's been under a lot of stress lately.'

To round off, Aszal concluded: 'I like you Jas, yes, but not like that. I'm not your boyfriend nor ever will be.'

That made me spin round. 'You' – I pointed at Aszal – 'could never be my boyfriend. I would want someone strong, who knew his own mind – not under the control of his mother. Yes, I know you like me, but you're too weak, so much so you make me sick.'

'Now come on, Jas, there's no need to be spiteful,' Andy said.

'Spiteful, spiteful. You lot call yourselves Christians, and you're so evil.' Tears began to run down my cheeks. 'You pretend to care for people but you don't. All that quoting out of the Bible, it's just words to you. And as for you Aszal, ever since I met you, you've been giving me the come on sign, well now I'm giving you a sign — drop dead!' I opened and shut the front door in a second. The bang was so loud I thought the house was going to collapse.

Walking down the road I could hear Cana calling after me. I ignored her.

'Jas, Jas, wait.'

I walked even faster.

I was angry with myself for not keeping my mouth shut. If I had shut up, Hina would have been the one with the black mark against her name. Instead I opened up like a volcano erupting. All those weeks I had managed to keep cool with Judy and now I had to spoil it by mouthing off Hina.

Cana caught up with me. We walked on in silence. Even on the bus we didn't speak. I couldn't even if I had wanted to: my lips seemed to be stuck together.

When we got home I was aiming to go straight to bed but Judy waylaid me.

'I want a word with you, Jas.' Looking past my shoulder, she said to Cana, 'And you, too.'

We went into the lounge.

'Well, what happened tonight? I have just had a frantic call from Andy who told me that you, Jas, had had words with Hina and then slapped her.'

Neither of us spoke.

'Come on, out with it.' She looked like a revolutionary with her feet apart and her hands on her hips — aiming to change the world.

Resignedly, Cana said: 'Jas and Hina just had a difference of opinion, that's all.'

'Why?'

'Oh, I don't know, Mum.'

121

Judy looked at me, I looked at her.

Suddenly I felt hot. From my toes up to my head. Not an actual burning sensation, but like when you're first exposed to the sun — it takes your breath away and then no area of skin is exempt from the hot rays. A rumbling in my stomach was slowly gathering momentum as it crept up to my throat. My ears were scorching hot, and my tongue dry. I knew that for all those weeks I had been keeping my mouth shut, now was going to be my undoing.

'Well?' Judy knew too that this was going to be a showdown.

'Well what?' I shouted.

'It's over Aszal isn't it? And don't shout at me, Jas, I won't stand for it.'

'Oh yeah? Then what are *you* going to do? Hit me?' I smirked at her.

'Would you speak to your mother like that?'

'Leave my mother out of this. You white women are all the same.'

'Jas, don't say that.'

'It's true. How you married a black person I'll never know. Underneath it all you're racist like the rest of them. You were lucky your children never came out too dark and — '

'That's enough. Now, young lady, while you're under my roof you will have to obey my rules and as from now you're grounded. You won't be going out anywhere. Understand? I won't be talked to like that.'

I laughed.

'You and your Christian values. What you would really like to do is give me the beating of my life, but if you did that you wouldn't be able to foster any more children and God wouldn't let you into heaven.'

Cana held my arm and tried to steer me out of the door.

'And for your information, madam, I love black people, Indian people, any people. I think you're the one who has the problem.'

I could see tears in Judy's eyes.

'Hit a sore point, have I? Liking black and Indian people wouldn't just be the men, would it?'

Judy took a step towards me and for a moment I thought she was going to hit me.

'If you don't get up those stairs now,' she said quietly but with a deadly menace in her voice, 'I won't be held responsible for my actions.'

'You've never liked me since I came to this house. Well, you won't have to suffer me any longer. I tell you what, I'm going right this minute, because if I don't *I* won't be held responsible for my actions, get it?'

I ran upstairs as though a monster with ten heads was after me. Going straight to the wardrobe I began to drag my clothes out and throw them on the bed.

I couldn't really see what I was doing, I was blinded by tears.

'I hate that woman, I hate that woman, I hate that woman.' I couldn't seem to find any other words to say.

Cana sat on her bed. 'Jas, stop. Why did you say those things to my mum? Do you know how much you hurt her?'

I could hear Cana sniffing. I knew she was crying and I didn't want to face her.

'Hurt her, hurt her. What about me?' I spun round at Cana. 'My mum's just had a major operation, I'm living with a bunch of religious hypocrites, some little tart tells me I've got the devil in me and Aszal thinks I fancy him.'

'Well, you did.'

'Don't you start, Cana. I thought you were my friend.'

'I am, but I can't lie. This is what it's all about. Aszal's rejected you and you can't handle it so you take it out on my mum.'

'That's not true,' I screamed.

'Yes it is,' Cana screamed back.

We faced each other like two wild animals.

As though reading my mind, Cana said: 'You had better not hit me, Jas, because I'll hit you back.'

123

I stared at her.

The door burst open. It was Aubrey. He had just come in.

'Right. You two — in bed and in the morning I want an explanation.'

I wanted to say something. Aubrey held up his hand. I closed my mouth.

Pushing the clothes on to the floor, I climbed into bed fully clothed.

Cana knelt down by the side of her bed.

Just before I fell asleep, Cana leaned over me and said she was sorry. I don't know what my answer was, my eyelids seemed to be coated in lead. I mumbled something incoherent and was out like a light.

What a day!

13

The cramp in my left leg was paining me so much I knew that I would have to get out of bed. But I didn't want to. Facing the Fentons (any of them — what affected one affected the lot) was something that I didn't relish.

Yesterday was vividly etched on my mind. So was the pain in my leg. I got up.

Going to bed fully dressed isn't a good idea, but it saves getting dressed in the morning! My jeans were in a terrible state, creased like a screwed up piece of paper, and my shirt was the same.

Sitting on the edge of my bed I felt like I had a hangover (not that I had ever had one, but the way I was feeling it couldn't be far off!).

I rested my elbows on my knees and cupped my head in my hands. The horrors of the night before came back like an enemy from the dead. Hina was the root of evil as far as I was concerned. I was glad I had slapped her. If I had any regrets about my actions yesterday, that wasn't one of them. Given the chance again I would probably do more than slap her. Arguing with Aszal was a bad move though. I wished I could turn the clock back and omit that part, but what was done was done. Strangely enough, I still liked him, but not as much as before. It had never entered my mind before to call him a 'Mummy's boy', but now I could see that I was probably right.

A deep groan escaped from me when I thought of what I had said to Judy. She hadn't really said anything horrible to me, just threatening, and that was only after I had pushed her on purpose. I wished she had been the one to say nasty things to me, instead of the other way round. Then it would have proved to me and everybody else that she wasn't a nice person. The way it stood now it was *me* who was the ogre!

It seemed impossible to apologise to her. I knew that I should, but I just couldn't see myself doing it!

My mum would go mad if she found out about this. Somehow I would have to make sure she didn't. If she did, I would have to put my side across strongly.

I went to the window and looked at the sky. This Saturday morning was going to be a good one (weather-wise!). The sky had hardly a cloud in it. I could smell the budding flowers from where I stood in the bedroom — well, almost. They looked good, anyway. It's peculiar how the world outside sometimes doesn't correspond with the feelings you have inside. There was a thunderstorm inside me. I hoped that I could keep the lid on it.

'Jas.' It was Matt.

That's all I need, I thought. Some stupid little boy to start me off.

I didn't answer him.

'It's your mum on the phone.'

I spun round.

'Why didn't you say?' I shouted.

He seemed a bit nervous. 'Hmm, I'm telling you now,' he muttered.

I stormed past him and, taking the stairs two at a time, I got to the phone in about a second!

'Hello Mum. How are you? . . . Great . . . I'm fine' — no need to say anything about last night — ' . . . What's that, Mum? . . . What? . . . Already? Well, I suppose you're right . . . How long for? . . . I see . . . Where? . . . That's a bit far . . . Will I see you before you go? . . . Now . . . Oh, Mum . . . Aunt Lyn, that'll be nice for you both . . . No, it's all right, Mum, we can make our own way

126

there, there's really no need, no, Mum . . . Okay, then . . . Hold on.'

Laying the phone down I called Judy.

'Judy, my mum wants to speak to you,' I said abruptly as she came out of the living room. I couldn't look at her, so with eyes lowered I made way for her to get to the phone and stood at the foot of the stairs. I wanted to make sure she didn't say anything to Mum. I wasn't sure what I would do, but when the time came I was sure I'd be able to think of something.

'Hello Hilary . . . How are you? . . . The family and I are great . . . Jas, she's — she's fine . . . No, no problems' — our eyes met over the receiver — ' . . . Are you really? . . . Oh, you do deserve the rest . . . Oh please don't think of it like that . . . We'll bring all the children for you . . . Hmm . . . We'll make it a day out, don't worry Hilary . . . I understand it's such short notice . . . Look, just take it easy, and remember we are praying for you . . . You would? Okay, we can sort that out another time. Bye for now, God bless you.'

Judy handed the phone back to me and at the same time she said: 'I want to speak to you after you've spoken to your mother,' and went into the living room, not even waiting for me to answer her.

'Hello Mum . . . Yeah, I heard . . . Okay then . . . Take care of yourself . . . I'll be all right . . . See you soon, I love you Mum, bye.'

As I put the receiver down it rang.

'Hello . . . Who? Oh Robert, what a nice surprise . . . I am pleased to hear from you . . . How you doing? . . . Great . . . When, today? Well I, eh, I'm not too sure . . . Of course I do, but — look, I have to sort a few things out here first of all . . . What do you mean you won't take no for an answer? . . . How did you get the address? . . . I gave it to you? . . . Oh yes, I remember . . . Okay, I don't seem to have any option . . . Yeah, three o'clock, bye.'

I can't complain of having a boring life. One thing seems

127

to happen after another. My mum had been offered a month's holiday with Aunt Lyn's family in Southampton; apparently they have a big house and are quite well off. Mum was going today. I would really have liked to see her before she went, but Aunt Lyn's husband Eric was going to drive them both down now.

Robert had invited me to see some friends of his playing in a group in a jazz club in Camden Lock. He was borrowing his mum's car and would pick me up at three. I hoped that by that time this little situation would be sorted out!

Outside the living-room door, I needed every ounce of courage I could muster to enter — I opened the door.

' . . . so that is why love is important, Dad, but I think love is easy.' Matt grinned as though he had just discovered America.

Aubrey looked up at me and said, 'Hi, Jas. Come and sit down.' Then he turned back to Matt and began to explain why love wasn't so easy.

'For us to love those that we are related to is no problem —'

'Oh yeah?' said Matt, looking at Cana.

Cana poked her tongue out at him.

'Behave yourselves,' Judy said.

Aunt Myrtle cackled. 'Mi know yu picknee love one anodder.'

Aubrey continued as though he hadn't been interrupted: ' . . . loving people who are good to us doesn't cost us anything, but to love those that we don't have any feeling for or are repulsive to us or are no use to us is another matter.'

The room became quiet. I felt so uncomfortable. Was this their way of telling me something?

If I was being told off in a roundabout way, then this was easier to handle than a full confrontation, but if it was the 'breaking in' of more to come I had better be on my guard. This family is weird, I thought.

'Yu know is true what yu sey, Aubrey. Mi remember a

time inna Jamaica when a woman name Mistress Brown and her husband catcha fight inna de yard. Him did have a next woman. She fling him out. Dis was when mi a little picknee.

'Much years later, mi did walk down town and dis dutty nasty man who nar wash since him born come and ask mi fi money — mi just come from church and did dress up. Mi did vex and ready to walk 'way from de man when him call:"Miss Myrtle, Miss Myrtle, mi know sey it yu?" When mi look good mi shock. "Mr Brown is yu?" "Yes, Miss Myrtle, is Mr Brown." "But yu turn tramp?"

'Him never answer mi. All mi could do was give him a little change mi did have. Yu know mi did feel so bad when him approach mi, him look so terrible and if him never did call mi name mi woulda just walk pass him and pay him no mind. And imagine mi just come from church. Hmm.'

'That's exactly what I mean. Loving the unlovable.'

Picking up the Bible from his lap, Aubrey began to read: 'The word of God says that "Love is patient, love is kind. It does not envy, it does not boast, it is not proud. It is not rude, it is not self-seeking, it is not easily angered, it keeps no record of wrongs. Love does not delight in evil but rejoices with the truth. It always protects, always trusts, always hopes, always perseveres. Love never fails."'

'Does it really say all that, Dad? That's hard,' Matt whined.

'You're telling me. How are we supposed to love during hard circumstances?' Cana said.

'God has equipped us by sending his Holy Spirit, that enables us to do and think things otherwise impossible in our natural strength.'

'Dat is true, Aubrey.' Aunt Myrtle nodded her head in agreement.

The armchair nearest the window had been vacant (whether or not it was deliberate, I was glad — I didn't want to sit next to anyone). I slipped my hands into the pockets of my jeans. I felt out of place. My clothes looked awful, I felt grimy and I wanted to have a bath. I knew I couldn't just walk out of the room and have one, though — it would only add fuel to the fire. I wanted whatever was going to happen to be over and done with as soon as possible.

I couldn't look at anyone directly, except for Aunt Myrtle who smiled broadly at me and I at her. I glanced secretly at the others. All of them barring Judy were caught up in the conversation. Judy sat looking from one to the other while they spoke or looked down at the Bible on her lap. I wondered if she was storing up her energy to let it loose on me. Or was she full of regret? That was very doubtful.

I yawned. I felt so tired: my bones were aching, my eyes hurt and my head was beginning to pound. Closing my eyes and thinking of nothing I must have dozed off.

'Jas, Jas.' Judy was shaking me.

Looking up at her standing over me, I immediately thought that this was it, Judy had turned to violence. So I leapt out of the chair like Superwoman ready to defend myself.

'What do you want?' I tried to shout, but it came out as a croak.

'It's okay, love, I'm not going to bite you.' She patted my shoulder. I shrugged her off.

'Sit down, Jas. We want to talk to you.'

Blinking my eyes to clear them, I stumbled back into my chair. I put my hand to my mouth to cover a yawn and looked round the room. Cana, Matt and Aunt Myrtle were gone. This was it.

Judy spoke first. 'I know what a difficult time you're going through, living amongst strangers and your mum's operation, but your behaviour last night had nothing to do with that. You were just being rude. Why?'

'You were being rude to me, that's why.'

'What do you mean by being rude?'

'Well, asking me my business, that's rude,' I said petulantly.

'Jas, there's no need for that tone of voice,' Aubrey said.

'It's true, though.'

130

'Would you speak to your parents like this?' Aubrey spread his hands out wide.

I lowered my head.

'Look, Jas, I'm trying to find out what the real problem is. Okay, last night tempers were flying high, but I think that this morning we should spend some time trying to find out what's actually the matter and how we can mend it.'

'Why are you doing this? Is it to torture me? Tell the truth, Judy. You don't like me and never have done.'

Our eyes locked.

Aubrey said: 'That's not true, Jas. Don't you think that it's more like you don't like Judy? And I suspect it has something to do with her colour.'

I sniffed. Being fenced in like this wasn't pleasant, to say the least.

'Well?' Aubrey obviously required an answer.

The night before I had been able to give it to Judy live and direct, but somehow on this bright morning the words seemed incongruous. Maybe my eyes were playing tricks with me, but sitting there together on the settee facing me, they looked good together. Oh well, I thought, I might as well get it over and done with.

'Yeah. I reckon that's it in a nutshell.' I suddenly felt in control of myself and together once I had said it.

Judy smiled. 'I knew all along, from the time I had picked you up and brought you here, that me' — she pointed to herself — 'being white had somehow put you out.'

'Yes, I could see that, too.'

I didn't say a word. I thought it would be better if they did the talking.

'Well, there's nothing I can do about my colour and I'm sorry it's offended you — '

'It hasn't offended me. I know a lot of white people and their colour doesn't offend me,' I butted in.

'Then what has?' asked Judy.

'I don't know, it's, it's . . .'

131

They both looked as though they were waiting to pounce on me.

I thought they wanted the truth so — here goes. I took a deep breath.

'I find it very strange that a handsome black man like you, successful and everything, couldn't find an equally suited black woman to share your life with. It's unfair, and a blonde woman is totally the opposite. Even if you had picked someone with black hair, maybe, just maybe, I could have understood, but, but . . . ' It sounded ridiculous even to me once I had said it out loud.

Aubrey laughed. 'You are not the first or the last person to be unable to understand our relationship. Listen, now. I love Judy and she loves me. It's that simple. We both believe that God has put us together and whom God puts together let no man put asunder — that means separate. It is not for you or anyone else to puzzle or concern yourselves with our business, but as you're living with us, I will talk with you about it, seeing as it is causing you problems. Love is a spirit. I don't think you can say to yourself that you will intentionally fall in love with so and so, it just happens. In our case I prayed so hard, because at first I didn't want to marry Judy, nor she me. Even though we are Christians, the colour issue can still be a problem, in the *church*. But God knows what He's doing, even if at times we don't. He was certainly right with us.'

He hugged Judy.

'Jas,' Judy spoke gently. 'Since I've been married to Aubrey, you can't imagine what I've been through. I've had people I have known for years reject me, people in the street call me names, the people on that side of the house' — pointing to the left — 'won't talk to us because of our mixed marriage and at church most people are fine on the surface, but at times some people have made slip-ups. It's life. I have had time to get used to it, but it's times like these when a young person like you rejects me, I find it hard to cope with and, and . . . ' She was close to tears.

132

This was something that I didn't expect. Shouting and screaming abuse at one another, that I could handle, but with this, tears and confessions, I was way out of my depth.

Aubrey put his arm around her and kissed her head.

I felt like crying. I did.

Both of them came over to me and hugged me, too.

'It's okay, Jas. We understand,' Aubrey whispered.

I wished I wasn't here.

Sniffing, Judy said, 'I'm sorry, Jas. I should've controlled myself more last night.'

Why am I crying?

'Even though we have had our ups and downs we feel you are part of the family.'

I'm definitely seeing Brenda on Monday; I want to go someplace else.

'You can stay as long as you want to.'

This is madness; they've cast some kind of spell on me.

'I think it's a good time now for us to pray that God will heal our hurts and mend our hearts.'

This is too much.

'Father God,' Judy prayed. 'Help us all at this difficult time to understand one another. Help us to love one another. Give us all that we need to overcome this situation. Help me, Lord, to love Jas as though she were my own child and that she can love or even like me too. Help us all, Lord, not to be against people who don't look like or behave like us. Help us to treat each other the same. Thank you, Lord, in Jesus' name. Amen.'

'I'm not racist, you know.'

Aubrey laughed out loud. 'We know that. Some young people have such definite feelings on certain subjects. Whether they get it from their parents or wherever, they just feel it so strongly that only time and experience can alter their way of thinking. Never mind, it's all part of life.'

Drying my eyes, I knew there was nothing more I could say but: 'I'm sorry Judy and Aubrey.' The words got a bit stuck in my throat but they still managed to come out.

133

I was pleased. If my mum ever found out what had happened she would kill me, then tell my father, who, when he came home, would kill me again! But I knew that once it had been resolved that would be the end.

'Right. There's something else I wanted to ask you, Jas,' Judy said getting up off her knees and sitting down. 'You like Aszal, don't you?'

Instantly my head came up and my mouth opened to deny it: 'No I don't.'

Judy smiled at me.

'Young people are always the same. Actions speak louder than words.' Aubrey grinned.

'Come on, this is a time of being truthful to one another. You do, don't you?'

It was pointless lying, so I just said: 'I don't like him as much as I thought I did. Last night killed some of it.'

'I hope it kills it all,' Aubrey said.

'Why?'

'Because,' put in Judy, 'Aszal's mum has had a difficult life. Aszal's her pride and joy and she watches over him like a mother hen. I don't think somehow she could cope with you as Aszal's girlfriend, and I don't know if Aszal could cope with being out of step with his mother.'

'I thought something like that was going on, she seems so cold. What about Hina, then?'

'Hmm, well, that's another matter. She happens to be the daughter of a very good friend of Aszal's late father.'

'So I suppose Aszal's mum would be happy if they got together?'

'Yes,' shrugged Judy, 'I suppose so.'

'Well, good luck to them. They suit each other as far as I'm concerned.'

'Anyway, is there anything else that we need to get out in the open? Jas? Judy?' Aubrey looked from me to Judy.

We both shook our heads.

'Right. Punishment, then.'

'Punishment? You're joking,' I said abruptly.

'No I'm not. You don't think we can just let you off like that?' smiled Aubrey.

'Okay, then,' I said cautiously. 'What is it to be?'

'Last night Judy said that you were to be grounded, and so I feel that we will go along with that and it will last for a week.'

'A week! But I've planned to go out with Robert this afternoon. He's coming for me at three o'clock!'

'You should really have asked us before you made arrangements.' Aubrey looked at Judy. They seemed to come to some agreement with their eyes.

'Okay,' Judy said. 'You can go with Robert today, especially as he's coming to pick you up. Who is he by the way?'

'He's someone I've known for ages and my mum and dad know him, he goes to college and — '

'All right, all right, we believe you and that he's okay, but that's it. No more concessions until the week is up.'

We smiled at each other in agreement.

Aubrey had just got up ready to leave the room when it suddenly hit me.

'Oh no!' I exclaimed.

'What's the matter?' Judy asked.

'It's the rap competition on Thursday.'

I looked at them both.

'Jas, we have just made an agreement about you being grounded.'

'But the girls and I have been practising for ages. We've got to do it.'

'We'll see,' said Aubrey. 'Right now, I'm starving. Let's have some breakfast.' He left the room.

Judy came over and hugged me. 'I'm glad we're friends, Jas.'

She left the room, with me walking slowly behind her.

Soaking in the bath after breakfast, I thought about the last twenty-four hours or so. It was really all so stupid — except

135

for the part where I slapped Hina: that was clever.

I had to admit I did feel differently about Judy, but to accept her fully — I didn't know if I could. There was more to it than her being white. It was Judy herself.

Being rejected by people had affected her somehow; well it was bound to. She made me feel uncomfortable. She seemed to go out of her way to be nice to everybody, but that was silly: how can you like everybody? It's impossible.

I know if you're a Christian you are supposed to love everybody, but in real life you can't. And Judy tried too hard, which resulted in your disliking her. It's better just to relax and let people accept you as you are, I thought. Maybe one day I'll tell her.

As for not doing the rap competition because I'm grounded! They are both sick. Even if I have to blast my way out of here, demolishing the house and killing everyone in the process — well, perhaps that's going a little too far. All the same, I'm going!

14

The Saturday before the rap competition, I went to Camden Lock with Robert. It was okay, nothing fantastic. He turned up in his mother's car, newly washed and polished. So I was a little impressed. He had on light-coloured trousers, a checked jacket, a white shirt and a tie. Where did he think he was going, dressed up like that?

I looked a picture — waist-length cable-knitted sweater, brown suede culottes, matching shoes and a white designer T-shirt.

As we drove along I told him briefly of the events of the previous night, omitting the bit about slapping Hina. Robert had a lot to say about mixed relationships, but what was so funny, when I thought about it afterwards, was that I ended up defending them!

'I think it's wrong for people of different colours or class or religion to get it together,' Robert said, rather patronisingly I thought, but I let him carry on. 'It causes too many problems for the children, for the people themselves and for society in general.' He smiled and looked at me. 'Also, in the case of white women marrying black men, it's all down to the slave days when the white women *made* the black men sleep with them or face execution. I know what I would have done in that situation. The thing is that it's a form of genocide on the black race, weakening the strain and all that.'

'Robert,' I interrupted at last.

'Jas?'

'You talk a load of rubbish.'

'You've been brainwashed. Anyway, I wouldn't expect someone of your years to understand.'

'It's got nothing to do with my years, but a lot to do with common sense. When you love someone, okay, you must like the way they look and dress and all that, but the bottom line is *love*. Whether or not you know what love is — that's what it all boils down to.'

Swerving to miss a three-wheeled car, he said: 'Is that what they' — he jerked his head back, obviously meaning Judy and Aubrey who saw us off — 'told you? That's not how it goes. He has money, right, good job, brains, good looks. What has she got? Blonde hair, full stop. She's no mug, but he is. Why couldn't he get someone of his own race? Let me tell you I saw that American model Beverley Allen on telly the other day and she is something else.' He kissed his fingers.

'When love hits you, come and tell me about it.'

Laughing, he looked at me. 'Yeah, I will.'

I said sarcastically: 'Even if she has blonde hair.'

'Don't get feisty now, Jas.'

The club in Camden was the pits: smoke everywhere and there must have been about two hundred people in a space that should only take fifty!

The group his mates were in could have done with some more rehearsals and a different lead vocalist! They were so amateur. It made me feel confident for our gig on Thursday.

After they had finished, they came over to our table for a drink. Robert flashed his cash-point card-holder and unfolded a twenty-pound note. He thought he was being cool. I knew he was being uncool!

He introduced them to me by name, and then he introduced me: 'This is Jas, my woman.'

It was out of my mouth before I could blink! 'You must be joking.'

His mates started to laugh.

It wasn't long before he took me home and when he dropped me off at the door he said: 'I'll call you sometime. How about the year two thousand?'

I laughed. Creep.

When I told Cana — she did ask why I was home so early — she said: 'The year two thousand. Some people say that's when Jesus is coming back.'

'Well, Robert had better call me before then.'

For about an hour each day after school BB, Lisa and I practised like mad. On Wednesday afternoon we missed school (there was no other way that I could have fitted everything in) and played through our songs what seemed like a hundred times.

I have never known a week like it. But in the back of my mind was the constant worry about whether Judy and Aubrey would lift my grounding ban.

I didn't want to discuss it with Cana. I felt that she would have agreed with me that I should do it, but she still had to see her parents' side of it. Besides, even though Cana and I were friends, I didn't feel a hundred per cent with her, wondering all the time, is she her mother's daughter?

Since the events of the last few days, or in fact from the time I had been living with the Fentons, I had changed. I felt different, like when you lose weight or cut your hair. I couldn't put my finger on how I was different. I just didn't feel me.

On Thursday morning I was up bright and early. I hung round the house waiting to see if Judy (Aubrey had already gone to work) wanted to speak to me. I had reminded her twice earlier on in the week about the competition and how important it was for me to go. All she would say was: 'Aubrey and I haven't decided yet.' It was the same today.

On the way to school, I decided not to go home afterwards, just phone Judy and tell her that I was going

139

to the competition whether she liked it or not.

I hate it when people think they have something over you and keep you hanging on a string. That certainly isn't good Christian behaviour!

After the first lesson at school, which was French (it could have been Russian for all the attention I paid it), Lisa and BB were outside my classroom door. Their faces were beaming, white teeth flashing brightly.

'What's happening girls?' I shouted, slapping Lisa's and then BB's outstretched hands.

'Cool, Jas, just cool.'

'We're gonna win,' grinned BB. 'I feel it so strongly, I just know that I'm right.'

We walked along the corridor together. The people around pushed past us, bumped into us but we didn't care.

'This is our big break. Today East London, tomorrow *Top of the Pops*!' cried Lisa.

BB stopped walking. 'You must be joking, Lisa. Top of the Flops, no way. I'm looking beyond that. It's the American Grammy awards for the "up and coming" new band. *Us*.'

We laughed at the top of our voices, heady from the excitement of our well-earned success.

The whole day passed so quickly. Mine was spent daydreaming.

I didn't feel any nerves at all until I got off the bus and was walking towards the Fentons' house. I had wanted to have rehearsals straight after school, but Lisa's mum had picked her up because she wanted to do her hair, and BB's cousin was helping her to get her outfit together, so I had no option but to go home.

I didn't want to face Judy, to be quite truthful. I was expecting her to say that she and Aubrey had reached a decision and I wasn't to be allowed to go.

I acted it out of my mind.

'So what's the verdict?' I asked, all laid back, pretending not to care.

'Don't take that attitude with me, Jas, it goes against you,' Judy shot back.

'Listen, woman. I really don't care what you have to say. I'm going.' Then I walked coolly out of the door with my stuff, not even giving Judy a backward glance as her voice, full of anger, called me back.

'Tough,' I shouted over my shoulder.

That was how I imagined it, but it turned out differently.

As soon as I walked through the door, Matt sprang on me like a cat on a mouse. 'Mum wants to see you, Jas.' He was grinning from ear to ear.

'Really?' I made to go up the stairs.

He tried to block my way. 'No, don't go up stairs yet. Mum's in the kitchen. She really wants to see you.'

I wasn't sure what to do. I wanted to go upstairs and get myself together before I spoke with Judy, yet at the same time I wanted to know if she was saying it was all right for me to go. My curiosity won.

I strolled nonchalantly into the kitchen. Judy immediately turned round from the kitchen sink.

'Hi Jas. Let me put you out of your misery, you can go. Aubrey and I aren't really heartless enough to stop you from doing something you have worked so hard and long for. I hope you win.'

Her eyes were twinkling.

I felt a bit choked. 'Thanks' was all I could muster. And turning round quickly, I bolted for the stairs.

Sitting on the edge of my bed, I felt strange. Deflation was more like it. I had geared myself up for battle and nothing happened.

Well, I had better programme my brain for success to get me in the right mood. I started going over the lyrics with the headphones on. I wasn't aware that Cana had come into the room until she waved her hand under my nose. I switched the tape off.

'All set?'

'Never more ready.'

141

'So Mum let you go after all. See, I told you she wasn't such a monster.'

'Whether she was planning to let me go or not, I knew that I would be going somehow.'

'You reckon? I could see that you were worried what Mum and Dad's decision would be.'

'Who was? I couldn't care less what they had in mind. I wasn't bothered.'

'Heavy words, Jas. Anyway you're going and so am I. I wouldn't miss your winning for the world.'

Cana saying those positive words gave me such a boost. I jumped up and hugged her. She hugged me back really tightly.

'You're going to win.'

I wanted to ask her to pray for me but felt stupid, so I didn't say anything.

Standing in the hall waiting for the cab (which Judy insisted I take and she was paying for), I felt tense. I caught her looking at me a few times which unnerved me even more. Matt was buzzing around like a pesty insect and Cana kept asking me if I was nervous.

'Where's the cab? It must be coming from Scotland.'

'Don't worry, Jas,' Judy said. 'It will be here soon. I think it would be a good time to pray before you zoom off, okay?

She looked at me. I nodded.

We held hands and Judy prayed. It was short.

'Dear Lord, please guide Jas in all that she does this evening. Make her way successful according to Your will. Let her do everything right and take away anxiety and fear. Thank You Jesus. Amen.'

A car horn burst through the walls of the house.

As we hurried out to the cab, Matt carried my things. Cana hung on to my right arm and Judy walked on my other side encouraging me to do well. She told me that before Aunt Myrtle had her early evening nap she had asked her to tell me that she had prayed for Jesus to bless me.

142

Sitting in the back of the cab my mind was like a tangle of spider webs.

Over and over again I kept thinking that Judy had actually prayed for me, and even before that she had told me straight out that it was all right for me to go to the competition. Wonders will never cease!

The cab pulled up outside the Metro, which was once the local Odeon, where the competition was being held. Helping me on to the pavement with all my things, the cab driver then pocketed the fare and jumped back in the cab and drove off. Lumping my gear up the stairs and into the dressing rooms was a bit exhausting.

Lisa and her mum and BB and her cousin were already there.

'We're gonna win!' shouted out Lisa, waving a lipstick brush in her hand.

I smiled.

'Too right we're gonna win,' said BB.

We spent most of the time in the dressing room, while the show was on. Now and again Lisa's mum went downstairs to see what was happening. The third time she told me she had spoken to Cana who said that she'd be leading the demand for encores when we did our thing.

'By the way, how is it at the house these days, Jas?' Lisa enquired.

'Fine.'

I couldn't have said that a few days ago, but 'fine' I suppose was the right answer.

Time flew by. Then there was a loud knock on our door followed by a voice announcing that we had five minutes. My bladder instantly filled up and my knees seemed to be giving out on me.

Lisa and BB seemed to be unaffected by stage fright.

'We're gonna kill 'em dead!' roared BB.

'Murder tonight,' shouted Lisa.

Lisa's mum and BB's cousin were laughing. I felt ill, but smiled all the same.

143

As we neared the stage we could hear the audience. They sounded like the crowds that attended the Roman gladiators' arenas — they wanted blood. The MC was having a hard time shutting them up.

Waves of sickness washed over me.

Lisa's mum happened to look round at me. 'You okay, Jas?'

Everyone's eyes were on me.

'Great, no probs.' I grinned revealing every single tooth in my mouth. It fooled them.

Why am I feeling like this?

I took some deep breaths. I prayed, or tried to. Desperation was bubbling up in my stomach.

Once on the stage, with the audience clapping and yelling, the lights and the heat made me feel a feeling that was so strange I couldn't put words to it.

BB walked to the front, grabbed the mike and just let the audience have it. 'You wanna move tonite?' she said with an American twang.

'YEAH!' roared the audience.

'You sure you know how?'

'YEAH' was the reply.

'Well let's go then.'

My confidence level soared through the ceiling.

We went wild. The audience clapped and danced and we gave it all we had. It was mind blowing.

I was full up inside with excitement, pleasure, every good feeling there is. As we neared the end of our song a thought flashed through my mind: I wondered if Aszal had turned up. I doubted it, particularly after the way I had slapped goose-features and mouthed him off. But just in case he was I really let myself go, to let him know that I wasn't bothered at him, or her for that matter.

When it was over, I staggered back to the dressing room exhausted. All my energy had been used on stage. I was drenched in sweat from my head to my toes, my heart was beating so hard I thought my number was up.

Lisa's mum had brought some refreshments. No sooner had I drunk a glass when a knock at the door told us we had to go back on stage to see if we had won.

All the acts were lined up and as the MC called each band forward the audience applauded according to how well they thought the band did. The band with the most applause would be the winner.

We were third from the end. The first five groups got really good applause.

Lisa and I looked at each other. Our eyes said: 'What are we going to get if these other bands did so well?'

Our turn. The audience went wild. Whistles were being blown and the clapping went on for what seemed like ages.

The group after us got nothing like as much applause. We must have won!

Then it was the last group's turn. If I had thought that we had a lot of applause I was totally unprepared for the reaction of the audience to this band. They went demented. They applauded all night with all the strength they had — well, it seemed like it.

The MC waved his arms about trying to calm the audience down. 'Okay, okay, we hear you people. I take it you have chosen "The Scratch-aholics" as tonight's winners.'

The audience started clapping again.

I wanted to leave — and fast.

'Let's give the other bands a round of applause and let's hear it from the top from "The Scratch-aholics", the hottest rap band in London.'

We waved and trooped off the stage.

Back in the dressing room BB was fuming. 'We should have won. The other group are rubbish. I've heard them before and we are easily better. They must've brought all their posse with them.'

I quietly began to pack up my things. I was feeling like a deflated balloon. I didn't want to talk to anyone.

Someone knocked at the door.

'Come in,' boomed BB.

Judy popped her head round the door. 'Jas?'

I looked up at her.

'Oh! Come in, Judy.' I didn't know what else to say. I was shocked to see her here.

'You were great, girls, I was so proud of you all. You had such confidence that you should have won it for that alone. Anyway, next time I'm sure you'll secure first place.'

'We should have won,' said BB.

'Well,' said Judy. ' "The Scratch-aholics" were good and they seemed to have a lot of friends along with them too.'

'You were right then, BB,' said Lisa's mum.

Holding her hand out to Judy, Lisa's mum introduced herself, and then there were introductions all round.

'Well it's a pleasure seeing such talent in girls so young. You must all come and see Jas as soon as you can, okay?'

Lisa and BB smiled and said yes.

Walking down the stairs with the noise of the speakers threatening to burst our ear-drums, I didn't know what to say to Judy. She was trying to talk above the noise but gave it up as a bad job.

Outside, Aubrey came up and took the bags out of our hands.

'Well done, Jas.'

Cana and Matt and his friend and Aszal and his brother and a few people I recognised from the youth meetings were milling around by the car. They all started speaking at once as I walked nearer.

'Well done, Jas. I didn't realise you were that good,' said Matt.

'Thanks,' I said, sort of sarcastically.

'No, really, you were good,' he insisted.

I looked up at Aszal just long enough to hear him say the same thing.

That night I couldn't sleep. We had lost the competition, yet I wasn't disappointed.

The fact that Judy and Aubrey and Matt and Cana and Aszal had all turned up to support me, especially after the way I had treated them, made me feel uncomfortable.

When we were walking down the path to the house, Judy had put her arm around me. I hadn't known what to do. The funny thing was, I hadn't minded as much as I would've expected. I couldn't put my arm round her though.

Later, as we sat in the kitchen drinking cocoa, I could sense that Aszal wanted to talk to me, but when our eyes met I just gave him a blank look. I didn't want to deal with him just yet, I had to sort Judy out first.

I turned over on to my side and listened to Cana's steady breathing. I had over a month left before I would be back home, and I would be nearly sixteen. There was no point in going somewhere else and having to start afresh getting to know new people. Staying here seemed the best thing to do.

I supposed I could put up with the crazy religious antics. The black and the white issue had turned out to be no big thing after all. The way Lisa's mum had responded to Judy — I had half expected her to refuse to shake her hand and say something insulting, but she didn't. In fact the opposite had happened.

And the way Judy so readily invited everyone to her house was impressive. She hadn't even met them before. At least it showed that she had manners.

The thought came into my mind that perhaps she was just trying to win over my friends. I pushed it out: Judy didn't have any reason to go out of her way and get all friendly with my friends, especially since I didn't have much time left here. No, she was being genuine. Hmm. This was certainly a turn in events.

I supposed that living with the Fentons had given me an insight into how mixed families lived. To be truthful it was no different from anyone else. That was a revelation.

Well, I thought, I must write more lyrics for the group, and we must keep going until we hit the big time.

I smiled. Snuggling under the duvet, I told myself it was about time (seeing that it was 2.30 a.m.) that my brain had a rest, my eyes were shut and I slept the sleep of the beauty.

School tomorrow. Some things just don't change!

I am not ashamed of the gospel, because it is the power of God for the salvation of everyone who believes.

Romans 1:16

For God does not show favouritism.

Romans 2:11

These quotations are taken from the New International Version.

If you have enjoyed this book, or have any comments to make, the publishers would be delighted to hear from you. Please write to:

Meryl Doney
c/o Hodder & Stoughton
47 Bedford Square
London
WC1B 3DP

GOLD BOOKS

A goldmine of excellent fiction for young adults, combining international award-winners and exciting new writers.

THE ARM OF THE STARFISH

Madeleine L'Engle

A quiet summer with a famous marine biologist turns into a frightening encounter for teenager Adam Eddington. Little does he know that his chance meeting with Kali Cutter on his way to Portugal will involve him in an unstoppable chain of events and an international conspiracy. As the danger mounts, Adam must make a decision that could affect the entire world − which side is he on?

'Tense, tricky, well-plotted, THE ARM OF THE STARFISH has all the stuff of which adult spy novels are made.'
The New York Times Book Review

A Canon Tallis mystery thriller, companion to THE YOUNG UNICORNS.

GOLD
BOOKS

THE BOOK OF THE DUN COW

Walter Wangerin, Jr.

At a time when the sun turned round the earth and animals could speak, Chauntecleer the Rooster ruled over a more or less peaceable kingdom. What the animals did not know was that they were the Keepers of Wyrm, monster of Evil long imprisoned beneath the earth. And Wyrm was breaking free . . .

'Belongs on the shelf with ANIMAL FARM, WATERSHIP DOWN and THE LORD OF THE RINGS.' *Los Angeles Times*

'A beautifully written fantasy . . . a book in which there is adventure and humour, betrayal and despair. But most of all there is hope.' *Washington Post*

GOLD
BOOKS

THE YOUNG UNICORNS

Madeleine L'Engle

The extraordinary appearance of a genie when Emily
rubs an old lamp in a junk shop is the first of several
bizarre events which turn into danger for the Austin
family. A sinister gang is plotting to rule New York
City with the aid of the powerful micro-ray. The
Austins uncover the plot and are forced to a
terrifying final confrontation deep below the city.

'A highly unusual novel, both frighteningly realistic
and highly imaginative.' *English Journal*

A Canon Tallis mystery thriller, companion to
THE ARM OF THE STARFISH.